Not In The Plans

HEATHER TULLIS

Also by Heather Tullis

Other books set in Juniper Ridge
Homecoming
The Carver Ranch series (Formerly Homecoming series)
Second Chances
Identity
Safe Haven

The DiCarlo Brides
A Perfect Fit
SEALed with Love
Reclaiming his Bride
Family Matters
Wild Hearts
The Last Bride
Getting Her Groom

In The Garden Series in Kansas
Hello Again
First Crush
Not in the Plans
Last Chance—coming April 17, 2018

Echo Ridge Anthologies
Christmas Kisses—One Winter Night
Kisses Between the Lines—Much Ado About a Kiss
Silver Screen Kisses—You've Got Email
Second Chance Kisses—Almost Home

Waypoint

Timeless Romance Anthologies
Spring Break-Dancing in the Flea Market
Valentine's Day—Deal Breaker

Not In The Plans

Book Three

In The Garden series

Heather Tullis

Not In The Plans

Published by Jelly Bean Press, PO Box 548, Osawatomie, KS 66064
ISBN: 978-1-63034-025-4

Cover design by Bill J. Justesen

Dedication

To Jesse: sometimes our destinations are not what we expected, but better than we could have imagined.
Leave a little room for surprises.

Chapter One

Jason McCormick was anxious to get to a woman who didn't love him. He glanced at his watch and then turned his beat-up Chevy toward the city office. He'd told Peter he would pick up the building permit for tomorrow's job, but he'd been at the lumber yard longer than expected and now the city offices were about to close. With any luck, Adelyn would still be there.

The air was clean and balmy after a spring rainstorm earlier in the day and he rolled down the window to breathe it in. He loved Kansas in the spring and the fresh air was especially nice after a long day of sanding mud off sheetrock in an office building downtown.

Letting out a breath of exasperation, he slowed at a red light and speed dialed Adelyn's cell phone number.

"Hi, Jason, what's up?" As usual, her sweet voice soothed and pricked at him at the same time.

"Are you still at the office?" *Please say yes.*

"I'm about to lock up. Do you need something?"

He tapped his fingertips on the steering wheel and stared at the red light, willing it to change while a single car puttered through the intersection. "The permit for the Parker complex. You do have it ready, right?"

"Of course. It's been sitting here since yesterday. How far away are you?"

"Getting close. I'm stuck at the light at the corner of Maple and Grove."

"I'll wait for you, then."

"Thanks, you're the best." Jason was relieved he had caught her before she left. Peter wouldn't have been happy if the excavator couldn't start the new project first thing tomorrow morning because they didn't have the permit to post on the property.

"I know. See you in a few." She hung up.

He eased on the gas as the light turned green, sliding the clutch back down as he shifted the truck into second gear. The fact that he'd get a chance to see Adelyn was enough reason to hurry on over there, even without the thought of keeping Peter, who owned Elliot Construction, off his back.

He glided into the parking lot four minutes after five and pulled into the spot beside Adelyn's car in the otherwise-empty stretch of asphalt. It was a good thing he'd called ahead. Had everyone left early for the Easter weekend? Like two days early?

She was waiting for him at the glass door, her blond hair coiffed back in a smooth bun on one side. She let him in and locked it behind him. "Lucky you called me. I'd have been out the door at five—it's been a very long day."

"They left you alone?"

"Just for the last half hour." She circled around the customer service window and brandished her key card to get into the office area. The place was perfectly ordered; her desk held only one piece of paper, which she picked up, along with her purse, which had been tucked out of sight under her desk. "We're short-handed because the schools are out for spring break and a couple people took vacation while their kids are free. Mandy and her family flew to Florida to spend the week at Disney World." She glanced at the space around her, then flipped off the light.

"Sounds fun."

"If you like that kind of thing."

"Who doesn't like that kind of thing?" He thought of Worlds of Fun only half an hour away and tried to remember the last time he had been there.

Joining him back in the foyer, Adelyn passed him the signed permit. "Everything is good to go. Despite Elliott Construction pulling out of the Indulgence Row project, they're still keeping you busy, aren't they?"

"Definitely. There's plenty of work to go around." Jason waited for her to lock up and walked her to the car, glad to have a few minutes to talk, even if that's all it could be. She was always so pretty and put together in her business suits and pearls. It was more appealing than he would have guessed before he'd started noticing them on her.

"Are you guys doing anything fun for Easter?"

"Coloring eggs and then Easter dinner. Mom has been looking forward to having a grandchild to spoil, and Felicia will fit the bill." Since his parents would become defacto grandparents to the third-grader when his sister married his best friend, Ben who was Felicia's uncle and guardian, in a few months, they were jumping into grandparenthood with both feet.

She shook her head. "Is Angelina going to make it home?"

Jason frowned as he thought of his youngest sister—she'd moved to New York City almost the moment she graduated from high school and apparently hadn't looked back. After seven years away, she'd not hit on any real success on Broadway, but she wouldn't consider coming home, either. "Angelina is always busy with something in New York. Someday maybe we'll get lucky and she'll grace us with her presence again."

Adelyn chuckled, her tones musical—had it always been that

way? He couldn't remember. He never noticed her like this when they were growing up and she, Piper, and his sister Maddie had been running in and out of each other's homes like they were community property. No, his fascination with her was much more recent. And ridiculously hopeless. She didn't even notice he was a man—he was just Maddie's family.

"Hey, are you doing anything Friday night?" she asked, pulling him from his wayward thoughts. "I mean, I know you aren't seeing anyone and it sounds like you guys aren't going out of town."

"Not really. What's up?"

"I wondered if you'd like to go out."

He nearly got whiplash, he looked over at her so fast. "You mean like a date?" Had he stuttered?

She looked nervous and embarrassed, gripping her purse strap tighter just below where it looped over her shoulder. "Well, sort of, I mean, Piper challenged us all to get dates, and the deadline is coming up for me and I don't know who to ask out, so could you do me a favor and go with me? Otherwise I'll be the idiot who didn't follow through and I hate that."

His heart went from racing double-time to thunking down into his boots. He should have guessed—of course she was only asking him out because she'd gotten desperate. Why else would she notice that he was datable? Obviously, she only thought of him as a convenience, someone to take for granted, and he didn't want that.

He needed to get a life. "You know, I don't think so. But good luck finding someone." He yanked open the door to his truck and slid inside, fuming—mostly with himself—for this pointless attraction he felt for her. Apparently, it was all one-sided.

Her eyes widened in confusion. "But why not? I mean, it wouldn't have to mean anything."

"I don't think that's what Piper had in mind." Any other

answer would be too revealing, and he honestly didn't need to deal with her knowing that he had fallen hard for her when he returned from Afghanistan a year and a half ago. The fact that he hadn't been truly interested in anyone else since was his own stupidity.

He might be in love with her. Maybe. But he wasn't going to be her pity date.

As Jason sat back in his truck, he wished he could figure out how to make her see him as something more than a buddy, but he had no idea where to start.

Adelyn watched Jason drive off in his truck, her brow furrowing as she settled in her sporty blue Ford Focus. What had that been all about? They hung out a lot, and she had helped him with the renovations at his house. So what was the deal with him turning her down? Was there something wrong with her so that he couldn't bring himself to go on an actual date with her instead of hanging out as friends?

She settled into the seat of her car—so different and less comfortable than the ergonomically correct chair she used at work. She had hoped Jason would agree to the date so she could clear the whole situation from her plate. Now she would have to ask out someone else. Why did dating have to be such a pain?

Chapter Two

Two and a half months later.

The community garden was in full swing and Jason was in the back, weeding beds and picking veggies. How had he gotten dragged into this again, he wondered as the sweat dripped from his forehead despite the fact that the sun would be setting in twenty minutes.

The humidity was reaching toward eighty percent and the temperatures still hovered at a life-sucking ninety-two degrees. After a long day of hanging sheetrock in this heat, he wanted to go home and drown himself in a cool shower. But there was Adelyn in her now-wilting office attire, sweat glistening on her face, and smiling as she talked with Maddie while they picked green beans. That made the heat and sweat worth it.

It had been over two months since she had asked him out while making it clear it was only her desperation talking, and though he'd been mad and she'd been embarrassed for a few weeks, they were long past that and back into their old groove again—which meant he tried to ignore his feelings and she was oblivious to them.

Could he be any more pathetic?

He pulled another weed and caught a phrase from her. "He totally didn't fit the list, so I kicked him to the curb."

List?

"Did it ever occur to you that the list could use some revision?" Maddie asked.

"I've revised it." Adelyn scowled at her.

"Um, I think revision implies changing some of the current content, not just adding more to it."

"What list?" Jason asked.

"It's nothing." Adelyn hurried to say.

Maddie shook her head. "It isn't nothing. It's this list of qualities a guy has to have for her to take him seriously as a romantic prospect. It's great in theory, but she's using it as an excuse to not get serious about anyone. Why do you think she's never had a boyfriend?"

Hadn't she? He couldn't remember—he hadn't been paying that much attention until a year and a half ago, but surely she'd had a regular boyfriend before that.

"I'm more discerning than most people," Adelyn said.

"I see, so I was happy to date just anyone—you know, before Ben and I got together—but you're *discerning.*"

"That's not what I mean, and you know it." Adelyn shot Maddie a look of reprimand.

Maddie's head tipped in acknowledgment.

"What kinds of things are on your list?" Jason asked.

"It's just your garden-variety list," Adelyn wouldn't meet his eye, very focused on the plants in front of her.

"Yes, totally," Maddie agreed with a false earnestness. "He will go shopping without complaint, trusts her to handle her own problems, will step in to help without being asked—"

"Wait, hold on—aren't those mutually exclusive?" Jason wished he could see the list, maybe it would make more sense than the way Maddie was telling it.

"Not at all—it's all about context," Adelyn said.

He didn't get it, but didn't argue. She had a list. He wondered what other kinds of things were on it, and how he could get a copy.

"You want to grab some dinner tonight?" the text message read.

Adelyn scowled. She had been trying to discourage Eric Sanders since they first met in March, but he wouldn't quit asking her out—it wasn't like he was an obsessive stalker, but still, every couple weeks he would find an excuse to ask her for dinner or a show. She wondered if it was time to move beyond polite refusals and lay her disinterest on the table for him.

Maddie's voice echoed in the back of her mind, saying that she ought to re-evaluate her list and give someone a chance. Was it weird that she made it to twenty-eight without a serious boyfriend? She ignored the screaming voice in her head that said yes, yes it was—especially when she didn't lack for dinner invitations. Was she too picky, or did she really attract too many of the wrong guys?

She tucked the portfolio with the—hopefully—final revision of yard plans for Jason to approve. He had been roped into hosting Piper and Reece's wedding in a little over two months, but the yard in his historic home was in serious need of an overhaul. She had been conferring with him and the deliriously happy couple to make sure it would meet their needs as well as be something he could be happy about maintaining for a good long while—if he stayed in the lovely place after he finished fixing it up instead of flipping it.

Either way, she hoped this would be the last round of revisions—they needed to get a move on with the work.

Adelyn lifted her hand to knock, but Jason opened the door before her knuckles could make contact.

"Glad you could make it. Dinner is on the table," Jason

gestured behind him through the kitchen that still needed an overhaul and into the freshly painted dining room. Things in here were certainly coming along, though far slower than she had anticipated. The kitchen and laundry room were all that was left to be done on the main floor and that was coming up next on the inside.

"What did you pick up?"

"DeQuan's. It's been a while."

It had, and the Chinese place adjacent to the community garden was the best in town. "Sounds great. We can go over the adjustments Comfrey and I made on the plant list and paths and eat some dinner. If you like the plan, we can go mark the lawn." Calling it lawn was a little generous, since that implied grass, rather than the patch of neatly trimmed weeds she had crossed through.

"Sounds good." He sat in the chair beside her and pulled a couple plates and cartons toward them. "You're not exactly dressed for this."

"I changed into more sensible shoes." She let her sandaled foot peek out from below the table. They were flats and very comfortable.

His brows lifted. "If you say so. At least you won't be walking on stilts out there." He helped himself to hearty portions of chow mein and orange chicken, passing the sweet and sour pork to her. She appreciated that he remembered her preference without having to be reminded constantly.

She felt her shoulders start to loosen from the stress of her job at the city as he talked about how things were going with his current construction job and the renovation he would be doing later with Charlee's construction crew. It was always comfortable and easy with Jason—far more than with most guys she was around. Dates were fairly torturous most of the time, which was the reason she kicked the guys to the curb, and not because she was too picky, like the girls kept telling her. She had her standards—who didn't?

"I'm glad things are going well for Charlee—she has worked so hard for this." Adelyn set her fork down, done eating. "You want to check out the plans?" She pulled out the portfolio.

Jason set his hand on hers and she tried to move out of his way. "Hey," he said. "No need to rush to that. Is something bothering you?"

Adelyn slid her hand away as her phone vibrated in her pocket. She pulled it out, grateful for the distraction. Eric again.

"Is something wrong?" Jason asked.

"Just a guy who wanted to grab dinner."

"You've already eaten."

"Yeah, it's not tonight he wants to go out. He's asked me out several times but doesn't seem to be getting the hint."

Jason nodded. "Was Maddie right the other day when she said you've never had a steady boyfriend?"

Never was such a harsh word. "Um, yeah. But that's because of bad timing and stuff. It's not a big deal." Except she was starting to wonder if maybe it was a big deal.

He studied her face for a moment. "You have a list of requirements for a man to reach?"

"Who doesn't?"

"I don't. No man, no how."

She chuckled. "You know what I mean—the purpose of dating is to figure out what you can and can't tolerate in a relationship. That way when you find the right person, you recognize it."

His brows lifted, but he didn't speak for a moment. "What other things are on your list? You know besides shopping with you and that contradictory will help without being asked, but trusts you to handle things yourself."

"I told you, those two are situationally relevant. For example, if I hire someone to come paint my house and they don't do the job right, I don't want someone to step in to try to fix it for me. I'm a capable person and can handle the conversation with the painter myself. But if I'm setting up for a friend's wedding, that's a big job and stepping in to help with the massive job would be completely appropriate."

"Okay, I get you now. What else is on your list?"

Adelyn almost didn't tell him—it was a little embarrassing, having him ask—and how did he remember the conversation so well at the garden? "You have to promise not to tease me about my list."

He had to pause, as if he wasn't sure if he could manage that, then nodded. "Okay, I promise—even if I have to cut out my tongue to avoid teasing."

She rolled her eyes, but accepted it. "The guy has to have goals—he can't slide by and figure the status quo is enough for him."

Jason grabbed the yellow legal pad he often kept handy for notes and scribbled on it.

Adelyn craned her neck to see what he was doing. "Why are you writing that down?"

"So if I see your perfect man, I can point him out to you, of course."

He spoke with full sincerity, so though something seemed hinky to her, she continued. "He looks out for what's best for me even when I'm not."

Jason paused halfway through writing that and stared. "Meaning?"

She sighed, hating to admit this. "I'm told I have a habit of being a bit of a workaholic. There may be times when I need to be reminded to step back and take a break, or whatever. He needs to recognize when I'm pushing myself too hard and point it out to me, that kind of thing. Not in a bossy or overbearing manner, but with kindness. I would do the same for him of course."

Nodding, Jason finished writing that down. "Next?"

"He needs to be open to new experiences, and I want him to introduce *me* to new things too—I'm not talking about taking me skydiving or anything—as interesting as that seems, I am *not* jumping out of a plane—but something different than my usual."

"Makes sense."

"There was the shopping one, and the two you said were contradictory."

"You can't remember the rest, or is that the whole list?"

"I'm telling them in order, otherwise I might forget them."

A grin lit up his face. "You have them memorized in order?"

"Are you going to make fun of me, or do you want to hear the list? Because we could go out and start work in the yard."

"Sorry, of course you know them in order." He added the three she had just mentioned to the list, though his smile didn't disappear. "Go ahead."

She considered refusing to go on, but the teasing had been minimal, so she continued. "He doesn't think that an offer of comfort, like a hug when I've had a bad day, has to lead to something more. Sometimes a hug is only a hug. And sometimes a back rub is only a back rub."

"This guy is supposed to be Superman, isn't he?"

"Give me a break—are you saying you can't accept that sometimes people just need a hug that isn't going to lead to intimacy?"

"No, but a lot of guys don't get that. You're right to have it on your list." His lips quirked as if he were holding back a smile.

Adelyn narrowed her eyes at him. "He needs to be able to have an adult conversation about feelings without trying to back out of it. He needs to be equally capable of wearing a suit and tie as wearing work clothes. I don't want someone who thinks one or the other is beneath them."

"Good solid middle-of-the-road guy. Gotcha."

"More like a flexible guy. He doesn't have to love going to city functions where we have to dress up, but I have to go sometimes, and he would need to come with me. It would be far easier for both of us if he was moderately comfortable in a suit and tie. But some of the guys I meet at those things don't know the first thing about physical work. They've never mowed a lawn or used a shovel and that's not what I want, either. I don't think my parents even have a hammer and screwdriver—if something needs to be done, they call for someone to do it. That's great for some things, but I want him to be able to do basic things, at least. Which leads to the next item—I want him to be good with his hands."

Jason grinned. "That could be interpreted more than one way."

Adelyn felt her face heat, and looked down at her food. When she had first written that, she meant it in the work form, but... "Both interpretations would fit."

"Likes me for who I am, and not the idea of who I am, or what I can get for him, and he doesn't want to change me."

"But you want him to introduce you to new things?"

"There's a difference between say, taking me to a rodeo, and trying to get me to change my wardrobe or my group of friends."

"Agreed." Jason scribbled a few more lines between bites of dinner, then pushed the list away. "That's quite a list. I noticed the list wasn't entirely one-sided—you want him to ...encourage you to grow as well as wanting someone flexible. How hard could it be to find someone like that?"

"Much harder than you might think. I dated a lot in college and the first couple of years after moving home so the list has grown over the years. I haven't been trying much lately, which is why Piper pushed me to get out and date someone last spring."

"Did you find someone for your date in March, then?"

She pushed a sliver of carrot around on her otherwise-empty plate. "Yes, but it didn't work out."

"He didn't want to go to the opera on his first date?"

"It wasn't anything formal. All we did was go to dinner, but he dominated the conversation talking about golf. Seriously, he didn't ask one question about me the whole night. Not again, thanks."

He grabbed the list and added to the bottom 15) Needs to know the difference between a conversation and soliloquy.

She was impressed, even if he was teasing her now. "Whoa. You know the word soliloquy. You know how to *spell* soliloquy. I'm truly impressed."

"There are all kinds of things you don't know about me."

Looking into his brown eyes, Adelyn thought he might be right about that.

It was more than an hour later when Jason said goodnight to Adelyn. They had reviewed the changes she and Comfrey had made to the plans and laid out the paths and beds with marking paint. She would be spending a lot of evenings with him putting everything into place, which suited him fine. Apparently he was a glutton for punishment.

He picked up the yellow notepad and looked at the list of items she'd mentioned her perfect man would need. He could be all those things.

Was he already all those things? He re-evaluated the list and thought back through the years, considering his past behavior. The only thing he lacked—at least that he thought she might have issues with—was being happy with his status quo. Except he really wasn't.

Not romantically, and not in his job. Why had he been

dragging his feet on both of them? He'd been working construction on and off since high school and had taken some classes in college that taught him about running a construction business.

He'd talked about branching out on his own, but instead, here he was, still working for Peter's construction company—which was now focused mainly on commercial construction. He did some work for Charlee, but she was focused on renovations. What he wanted to do was build custom houses, to help someone realize their dream in a new home.

Sure, he'd waited before because he knew he could get called up at any time, but he'd been back from his last deployment for a year and half, and been out of the Army for more than a year, and he still hadn't done anything about it.

He looked at the notebook again to re-read the list. Maybe it was time he pursued the things he wanted most instead of letting them slide. If he wasn't happy with the status quo, there was no one to blame but himself.

He knew which of the items on her list to check off first. The others were going to take a little longer to prepare.

Chapter Three

Adelyn adjusted her straw hat to cover her face better as the summer sun beat down on them. This was the third nursery she and Jason had been to that morning and the back of his truck was nearly full of plants.

"I can't believe they don't have pawpaws." Jason turned and gave her a quizzical look. "What are pawpaws again?"

She saw the teasing glint in his eye. "I guess you'll never find out." She was a big fan of them and had hoped they could put a tree in his backyard—she would pick the fruit if he didn't want it. The one time she had gotten her hands on the soft fruit, she had fallen in love with the custardy texture and light sweetness. They grew well in the area, but were hard to find and had too short of a shelf life to buy in the store. She would have to do some searching online for a tree.

"The ground isn't even ready to plant yet."

"It will be before you know it. Come on, let's check in the back. If they don't have the clematis back there, then we'll try again when it's time to pick up annuals. I wonder if they would order a pawpaw tree for us?"

"It's a good thing Reece is footing part of the bill."

Jason must not have done any research into the cost of landscaping before now because he'd been surprised at the over-all budget she'd proposed and had gritted his teeth at a few of the prices, though he hadn't complained about taking all morning to hit the various nurseries.

"Lucky you." Reece had called it a rental fee, but seriously, they could have gotten much cheaper rent at another location—what Piper wanted, Piper got, though. It was lucky for Reece that her wants were few.

"How did you get roped into helping with this, again?" Jason asked.

"I volunteered. I love your yard—or at least I love what it could be. I know what I would want if it were my house, and I think we can make it a great place regardless of who lives there after you finish fixing it up."

"Are you mentally selling it for me, too?" he asked as they passed a selection of evergreens.

"No, I wasn't sure if you planned to flip the place or stay there."

"I'm not sure yet, either." He stopped in front of a tropical climbing bush. "This is pretty."

"Yes, and it has to come inside during the winter or be replaced next spring." She flipped over the price tag and showed it to him.

He winced. "Yeah, I don't think I need to pay that much for one season. I'd probably forget to bring it inside, or to water it if I did bring it in."

"That's okay, we have everything planned out for you. Easy maintenance and lots of color were the watchwords." They stopped at the next row of staked plants and she searched through, grinning when she saw purple flowers opening on one of them. She double-checked the tag. "Clematis. Perfect." She searched through the other plants and found one more with purple flowers and Jason loaded them into the low wagon.

"Have you thought about buying your own place?" Jason asked.

"I'm sure your parents have been pushing you to move into one of those sleek apartments going up on the east end of town."

"They have, yes. They don't like my neighborhood, but I don't want a more expensive lease, and I haven't decided about a house yet. I'm saving up, though." She nearly grabbed some tall dark grass as they walked past, but held herself back. That would come later. Patience.

"I've thought about building," she continued. "But I can't decide. I'll figure it out later. For now I'm setting some money aside. I'd like something old, with history, like your house, but it seems silly for me to buy something so big. It's just me."

"You think I shouldn't have bought something so big?" Jason asked.

"I didn't say that."

"No, but that's what you meant, isn't it?"

"No. You're fixing it up. You might turn around and sell it at a nice profit—that's a business decision. Besides, someday you'll get married and have kids, so if you don't sell it, you'll put all of the extra space to good use." She stopped in front of a display of shovels and rakes.

Jason pulled a hand trowel from the wall and added it to their wagon. "I have everything else. You'll probably want something this size for planting smaller things, though, right?"

"Yeah." She noticed he hadn't commented on her observation about marriage and realized he hadn't really dated anyone since he'd been home from Afghanistan. Or was he dating and she didn't realize it? "Are you seeing anyone?"

Jason's head turned slowly her direction, his eyes narrowed. "Why do you ask?"

"Just curious. I've been thinking about signing up for one of those online dating services. Maybe Maddie and Piper are right about me being too picky."

"Now, out of the blue, you're going to sign up for a site like KCMeets? I didn't think you had any trouble finding guys to date."

"I don't. They're just all the wrong ones." She paused at the end of the checkout line. "Maybe I'm only discouraged. That can happen when your best friends both get married." Especially so close together.

"Maybe you need to keep your criteria, but think outside the box," he suggested.

Adelyn stared at him for a minute. "I don't think I understand what you mean."

His brows lifted. "Think about it for a while. You're smart, you'll figure it out." He pulled the wagon forward as the people in front of them paid and started loading things onto the counter.

What was with the cryptic answers? Keep her criteria but think outside the box? Maybe try dating guys she wouldn't have considered before? A few faces flashed across her mind. That was fine, in theory, but she still needed to be attracted to the guy, didn't she?

Adelyn put that out of her head. KCMeets along with the good and bad sides of online dating would still be there after she finished her time with Jason.

Maybe she should convince him to join too? He could stand to date more.

When something inside her said that was a terrible idea, she decided not to suggest it.

Adelyn watched Jason as he maneuvered the bucket on the mini excavator he had borrowed from Elliott Construction. The first couple of minutes were a little choppy, but then he settled into the machine as though he had spent a hundred hours in it.

Maybe he had.

The scoop slid through the grass and topsoil like it was cutting through sand, neatly staying between the lines they had drawn Thursday night to delineate beds they would be planting into, and the new paths they would be installing. Adelyn was starting to wonder if they had bitten off more than they could chew—this wasn't going to be a small project, and he did still have a complete kitchen remodel ahead of him this summer. Not to mention their full-time jobs.

Jason stretched his arm forward to pull the handle that lifted the balancing blade behind the excavator and then backed up, reset it, and took another bite with the scoop, expertly dumping the soil where they wanted it for later. She should be bored, watching him work, but she wasn't—there was something very manly about running a piece of equipment that powerful.

Jason connected the paths together and led them down to the pond they would be putting in, then set down the scoop on the ground and turned to her, waving her over.

She stepped closer and he yelled over the motor, "Hey, you want to give it a try?"

"What? No, it's fine." She was bound to break something.

He took her hand, shooting her a look that said he thought she was being a chicken. "Come on, it's easier than it looks. Besides, you won't damage anything major—this is the pond hole anyway."

Adelyn considered for a moment, anxious about the offer. "It looks complicated."

"Come on, you can do hard things." He gave her hand a tug. "I thought you wanted to be introduced to new experiences."

She bit her lip, then, on impulse, joined him in the open cab. He was right, she did want to try new things. How hard could it be, anyway?

Jason spread his legs to make room for her on the small seat and patted between them. "Just for the first minute while I show you how it works."

Adelyn only hesitated for half a minute–it wasn't as if Jason was going to put the moves on her. "Right. Okay." She sat down and placed her hands on the two controllers.

Jason slid his big, warm hands over her own, walking her through the controls–they each worked two ways to manage the excavator arm, lifting and squeezing closer, turning and scooping. He walked her through the process, his voice barely understandable in her ear, a low rumble amid the noisy machine as she dropped the scoop and it dug into the soil. She lifted it and the whole machine rocked a little, making her scream in surprise.

Jason chuckled, causing shivers to run up her spine. "It's fine. You're doing fine. It can be a little unnerving sometimes, but you aren't going to overturn it or anything. Shift the scoop to the left to dump it." He lifted his hands off of hers and set them on his knees to give her free rein–which was a little terrifying. She reminded herself that he had confidence in her, and she used that to boost her own confidence.

Adelyn felt her heart pounding as she nudged the control to the left a few times, jerking them with every movement. Then she used the other control to unkink the scoop and drop the dirt where they wanted it.

"You did it! See how easy it is?" Jason asked.

"I don't know if I could do this all day. I might have a heart attack."

"Nah, you'll catch on to it in no time. Try it again."

With his chest warm against her back and his musky cologne swirling around them, she did. After a few loads, Adelyn was surprised that she managed the scoop without too much trouble, though she still wasn't nearly as good as he was.

When they had most of the depth, she hopped down and Jason resumed the controls, cleaning up the edges of the pond and taking two more thin slices of sod from the end of the path before driving the excavator back onto its trailer.

"I can't believe I did that," Adelyn said as he came down to the ground again.

"I can. You're a natural. Maybe I should hire you to be on my crew."

"I thought you did framing and that chalky board stuff."

"Sheetrock. I do, but I decided it's past time I got my contractor's license. I've been working for Elliott Construction long enough, don't you think? It's time I branched out for myself."

"That's great. Do you have a job lined up?"

"Not yet. I still need to sit down and do the paperwork for licensing and figure out a business name and logo. You wouldn't happen to know someone who can help me cross the t's and dot the i's for my city license, would you?" He flashed her a grin.

She grinned right back. "I might. It seems like only a couple weeks ago I was walking through all of that with Charlee. I can't believe it." Excitement rushed through her, as it always did when someone talked about opening a new business in the city—working with businesses was her favorite part of her job at the city. "Where are you going to put your office?"

"Here to begin with. I won't be able to rent any space until I at least have a customer. This will cut way back on the overhead."

"I might know someone who's looking for a builder. Let me check and I'll get back to you on that. Are you thinking cookie cutter subdivisions?"

"I'll start anywhere, but honestly, I want to get into custom homes. I love the idea of taking the home owner's vision and helping them get exactly what they need. I still have to talk to the guys on my crew to see if any of them want to join me, or if they want to stick with what they're doing for Peter."

"It's a big change, with about a hundred steps, but you can do it." She'd seen him make it through so much, she knew he was up to any challenge. "Hey, Victoria's still trying to rope a couple more guys into the bachelor auction later this month. She's all about getting business owners in on it. You interested?"

"Not even a little bit. Not even if you promised to bid on me so I wouldn't have to go out with some crazy woman."

"Oh, come on. There must be something I could say or do to convince you."

He shook his head, sadly. "Not that you'd go along with. It's not happening."

Adelyn wondered exactly what his requirements would be, then decided to take him at his word. She wouldn't win points by pushing and he could be extremely stubborn. "Fine. I won't suggest your name." She checked her watch. It was nearly dinner time—they had spent the entire day together but she was itching to get a few of these plants in the ground before she headed home for the night. She was covered in sweat and stickiness anyway, right? What better time was there?

"How about if we plant the trees tonight, and then we can work on the other bedding plants after work on Monday?"

"You're a slave driver."

"Yep, that's me. Honestly, we have the plants—if you don't want to have to water them with a hose every day while we're wasting time, the sooner the better, right?"

"Sure. Remind me how I got conned into going to the nursery this morning instead of next week when the ground was ready?"

"My sparkling personality. Besides, the nursery had a great sale today."

He didn't argue, just headed for the shovels they had propped against his detached garage.

Adelyn may have felt a little triumphant, but if she did a little dance of joy at getting her way, she made sure to stop before he turned back to face her.

Chapter Four

Unlike Maddie's family, Adelyn's didn't meet for Sunday dinner every week. Adelyn's mom, Michele, liked to say it was weekly, but it varied from every other week to sometimes less than once per month depending on her social schedule. Because of this, Adelyn felt like she needed to attend when her mom had a family dinner, even though she would rather stay home most of the time.

She liked her mom's new husband, Clark, but seeing him only reminded her that Michele had never been able to find love permanently. Neither had her dad for that matter. It made it a lot harder to risk her heart after having seen the way that they had lived their lives and exchanged relationships like car leases.

She should be generous, after all Michele and Clark had been married for four years now. Even more amazing, they still seemed happy. She just wished her mom would be happy letting Adelyn live her own life.

The front door was always locked when she arrived so Adelyn knocked as usual. She didn't have to wait long before Michele opened the door to let her in. As usual, Michele was coiffed within an inch of her life, her bottle-blond hair had recently been trimmed back to chin length with perfectly smooth locks framing her face.

"Hello, darling, isn't that a nice outfit? What have you been up to?" Her tone and expression said that the outfit was anything but nice and Michele couldn't have been less thrilled with her appearance. Adelyn smiled and pretended she didn't understand the tone of her mother's voice. And that it didn't sting as much as it had when she was a child.

"Thank you, Mom. You look as lovely as ever. How is Clark?" As she entered, Adelyn noted the perfect order of the front room with the Baccarat candlesticks and vases of flowers in their standard locations. They continued past the music room with its Aubusson rug and baby grand—which no one in the family could play—and then into the kitchen area, where great smells had been wafting toward them. A loaf of French bread from the store sat on the counter, salad greens from the bag was already tossed with a few chopped tomatoes on top and when her mother opened the oven door to check on the lasagna Adelyn spied the box from the grocery store in the recycling. Her mother had never learned to cook, at least not the way that Eve McCormick did, but she always made sure that dinner was a nice experience, and that was nothing to sniff at.

“Clark should be here soon,” Michele explained. “He was out playing golf with one of his work contacts this afternoon, but texted that he is on his way home. How are things going for you at work?"

Adelyn tried to fill the time with discussion about recent decisions made at city council meetings that her mom hadn't paid any attention to. Then she moved on to talk about Maddie’s and Piper’s weddings and the project she was involved in with Jason to get his yard ready.

"That sounds like quite a project," Michele said. "When are the weddings?"

“Late this summer for Piper. I haven’t heard an official date for Maddie yet," Adelyn said. "I have my hands full dealing with the flowers and physical arrangements for the garden where the weddings will be held. I need to figure out bridal showers for both of them as well. I've been thinking about doing a joint shower."

"Oh, let me help with that!"

Adelyn was stunned. Her mother wasn't overly fond of either of her friends, but especially didn't approve of Piper and her colorful background—a background that made Adelyn prouder of her friend every day. She had overcome so much. "You don't have to do that."

"But I want to. You already said that you have your hands full preparing for the weddings, and this is such a small thing. You know I can throw a great party. I'm already getting ideas for decorating and games as we stand here. Don't you trust me?"

Not entirely trusting that her mother would give a shower that would reflect the bride's tastes was beside the point. It would be lovely and tasteful, and no doubt the exact kind of party that her mother had been longing to throw for Adelyn herself for years now. But she rarely involved herself in Adelyn's circle of friends, and it was nice to think of having her mother's support, plus having the lion's share of the work for the party taken off her hands.

All of this flashed through Adelyn's mind—hopefully fast enough her mother hadn't noticed. "That would be great. We can set up the basic plans together, to make sure that the party will reflect the brides' tastes, and then you can run with it. Only Comfrey asked to provide the party favors, so you'll need to make sure that we get a final head count early on."

"Hmm, that would be fine, I suppose. We'll have to sit down tonight and pound it all out after dinner. Piper's wedding is less than two months away." Michele shook her head. "Who ever heard of rushing to the altar like this anyway?"

"Mom, don't you remember what it's like to realize you've found the one you want to be with forever? They've never been so happy."

"I wish you would find someone like that," Michele said. "You know I met this very handsome young man the other day—"

"No, Mother. I am not interested in dating your friends. I'll find my own man." Adelyn was sick of this discussion, they had been having it ever since she returned home from college. Her mother hadn't been interested in her dating at all in high school and had discouraged it while she was studying in college, stating that early relationships were why she had ended up married to Adelyn's father. However, as soon as she graduated, her mother had been all about Adelyn finding exactly the right man and settling down.

"Honey, I had already been on my second marriage by the time I was your age," Michele said.

"Yes, but I don't want to marry four times. I'd rather only marry once. I'll wait for the right man." Adelyn picked up the bread knife off the counter and began slicing the French bread for the garlic seasoning that was sitting nearby. She felt a twinge of regret for saying something so mean almost before her mouth had closed.

"You don't have to rub in my face that I made some bad choices with men before I met Clark. If I hadn't, you wouldn't be here."

Adelyn's father had been husband number one, and nearly number three as well, when Adelyn had been a pre-teen. Thankfully her parents had realized it was a mistake before they tied the knot again. It had still broken her heart, but with hindsight, Adelyn could see that it would've been worse in the long run if they had married. It had been bad enough dealing with the second breakup without the custody battles all over again.

Now she did all she could to avoid having them in the same room at the same time. She was really glad that neither Piper nor Maddie had to deal with that at the weddings—though there would still be fun family dynamics aplenty for both.

"Are you dating anyone?" her mother asked.

"I date." Adelyn kept her voice as even as possible while she focused on buttering the bread she had just sliced.

"Darling, there's a difference between dating now and then and having a relationship. It's about time you settled down and got married too don't you think? Is there anyone in particular that you've been dating? Maybe that cute but single councilman I've seen talking to you at city celebrations?"

The back door opened and Clark announced himself as he came down the back hall toward the kitchen. "Hello, honey. I'm not late, am I?" Clark was nearly ten years her mother's junior and full of vitality–not that her mom was old, but Adelyn sometimes wondered what had made Clark interested in her instead of the younger women that must have flocked around him. Then again, what brought any two people together? She didn't have any room to speak since she wasn't exactly the poster child for healthy relationships. She turned and smiled to Clark, greeting him as he entered.

"Hi, we're about ready to eat," Michele said. "Could you please set the table?"

Clark approached her for a quick kiss before opening the cupboard with the dishes. He began setting things on the counter, but it wasn't until he had picked up the plates to put them on the table that Adelyn realized a fourth person must be joining them. "Mom, did you invite someone extra for dinner tonight?"

"Yes, didn't I mention it? He should be here any moment."

Adelyn managed to hold in the groan that bubbled up her throat, although it was a near thing. "I told you I don't want you setting me up with people."

"Adelyn, I'm not setting you up with someone, I invited this nice young man who happens to be single to join us for dinner. All you have to do is to be kind and friendly and hold scintillating conversation with him as you usually do. If nothing happens then nothing happens. I thought it would be nice if we had another visitor to make things a little bit more interesting."

Adelyn was mortified. Seriously? Didn't her mother understand yet that Adelyn wanted to figure things out for herself?

The front doorbell rang. Great.

A moment later, mom brought back a man who was probably older than Clark, and all smiles. Adelyn had never seen him before, which was a surprise, since she saw many different faces come through the city offices. He must not have a business of his own in town, or she would know him. She smiled and greeted him, wishing she could sneak out the back door and go home. Too late now though, so she might as well face it.

And if she made it through dinner without wanting to bash her head against the table a few times, she would consider it a success.

Chapter Five

Women in Business meeting was abuzz with the upcoming bachelor auction. Adelyn couldn't believe some of the men Victoria had managed to line up for it—including Matthew Craig, the city councilman Adelyn had gone out with once in the spring.

She hung around as most of the other ladies filtered out, headed back to their businesses—she had to talk to Victoria before returning to work herself.

"We look forward to seeing you there," Victoria said to a woman Adelyn vaguely remembered from another Women in Business meeting.

"And what can I do for you?" Victoria asked when she noticed Adelyn. "Are you planning to bid on a bachelor at our auction?"

Adelyn chuckled. "Too rich for my blood, no. But you said you still need volunteers, and I'm available that night."

"Perfect. I'm having the staff wear cocktail gowns or something similar—the whole event is supposed to be classy. You have that look down, and I'm sure you have a dress or three that would work?"

"Of course. What time do you need me there?" Adelyn got the details about the evening and entered them in her planner, then headed to work.

The bachelor auction seemed a little medieval—in the reverse, of course—but it was going to raise money for autism which was definitely a worthy cause, and it gave her an excuse to dress up, which she always enjoyed.

It had her thinking—again—about dating. And how she wasn't. Maybe she should give this online thing a try. Darla, the city accountant, had met her husband online and they seemed very happy, even after ten years. If nothing else, it would either confirm or do away with her list.

Summer had officially arrived—even if the calendar said it was more than a week away still—and it was hot as she walked back to work. She was at her desk so much that she took advantage of every chance to get up and move on her breaks, but she was starting to second-guess that decision this time.

Exercise was great, but showing up for work sweaty was another issue entirely.

Adelyn greeted Mandy, a pleasant woman in her mid-thirties, at the front office and used her key card to move into the back offices. She detoured to the bathroom to touch up her hair and makeup before returning to her desk. She would be calm, friendly, and helpful—that was her goal with every business interaction. It was the Shaw way—she just chose to do it in the city offices instead of as a business mogul like her father had wanted.

After answering email and returning phone calls, she went online to pull up the forms for Jason's new construction company and sent him links through his email. There was a lot to do when you set up any business, but construction had its own set of rules and guidelines on top of it all. If this was something he wanted to do, then she would help him as much as she reasonably could.

She didn't bother lying to herself that she would do the same for anyone—she had done it in the past, but only if they asked. Jason hadn't asked for help, but they were practically siblings, growing up together all the time. She would do the same for anyone in her group.

Thinking of the community garden group, she flipped open the notebook she used as her planner and double-checked the next work date. Not until Tuesday night—that meant she would have time to help Jason in his yard that night. She picked up her cell phone and sent a text asking about his schedule, then answered her desk phone. No rest for the weary.

And she was perfectly happy with that.

"So, Adelyn, date anyone recently?" Piper asked.

"You and Maddie are obsessed with making sure Comfrey and I date." It was their weekly girls' lunch—which was far less than weekly during the school year when Maddie couldn't get away from her students.

"We just want the same happiness for you that we've found for ourselves." Maddie ate another thick-cut steak fry.

"I'm happy." Adelyn considered happiness to be a state of mind for most people—unless you had a medical condition like depression—you pretty much decided how happy you were going to be and made it happen.

"You know what I mean. Have you ever thought about online dating?"

"I've done that," Comfrey said. "I even went out with a guy for a while, but it didn't work out. Then I got too busy with my permaculture business and didn't want to deal with the guys on the group I signed up for."

"See, they're all weirdos," Adelyn said.

"No... well, okay, some of them. But honestly, most of them were just nice regular guys. Too regular for me, honestly. I need someone a little off the beaten path." Comfrey finished her veggie burger and washed it down with sweet tea.

"I thought you said you wanted a regular guy?" Piper said.

"I said the guy at the nursery wasn't conventional enough—I didn't say I wanted to marry an accountant." She paused as if to consider that phrase. "Well, not unless he also has some traits that make him a bit more interesting than the average. I want a hybrid." She brought her hands together like the binding of a book in illustration.

"What does that leave—online dating?"

"You might as well set me up with a matchmaker," Adelyn protested. "No doubt that would be just as effective."

"I actually know one of those." Comfrey calmly plowed through her side of steamed broccoli. "One of the women from the shelter group used to work with a matchmaker. I'm trying to convince her to set out on her own."

"How is that any different than online dating profiles?" Adelyn asked.

"It's more personal. You'd be surprised at how successful a good matchmaker can be—not one of these fly-by-nights, mind, but someone who really has a knack of understanding people. Though even those can miss sometimes." She looked down at her plate as her lips pursed. Clearly there was a story she wasn't sharing.

Adelyn was about to ask when Maddie pushed back her plate, which still had half her fries on it. "Okay, this has to be the last lunch here until after the wedding or I won't fit in my dress."

Though Adelyn wanted, desperately, to ask about Comfrey's experience, she accepted the shift in subject—Comfrey wouldn't talk until she wanted to. "You haven't even picked out your dress yet. Or set a date. Speaking of which, what were you thinking, time-line wise?" Adelyn had considered becoming a wedding planner when she was in college, but in the end decided that she wasn't a big fan of bridezillas. Her job for the city wasn't as creative most of the time, but it had a lot of other things going for it.

Helping her friends with their weddings was a great opportunity to use the party-planning skills her mother had helped her hone over the years.

"We were talking it over. I have to start showing up at school to prep my classroom on August fifteenth, and after that things get dicey."

"Are you talking about waiting until Christmas break?" That would give them a lot of options, but the alternative...

"No, we're talking about August third." Maddie waited for the gasps of surprise to subside. "I talked to Jason last night about using his backyard as well. I love what you're doing with it. I figured we could add some pots with different colored flowers and dress things up so it'll look different than for Piper's wedding."

"That's less than two months. You could take a week off during the school year instead," Adelyn suggested, even though she was already thinking about how to tweak the yard to suit her friend's personality while still making it easy to redress for Piper's wedding the following week.

"You wouldn't mind if I cut into line ahead of you in your wedding venue, would you?" Maddie asked Piper. "I don't want to step on your toes."

Piper laughed. "Not at all. We can work out all the kinks on your wedding so *mine* will run more smoothly."

That made them all chuckle and they settled in to discuss plans for Maddie's wedding. Adelyn would have to talk to Jason about shifting the time line, and then she'd have to figure out how to customize the setting for each of the weddings without doubling the work load.

"You need to get the basics picked ASAP so we can figure out the logistics," she said to Maddie.

"You available to talk it over tonight?"

"I was going to meet Jason to finish planting everything we bought on Saturday. He needs to build the lattice and pergola before we can pick up anything else."

"Great, I'll join you to help and we can talk plans. I have dinner in the Crockpot—it's plenty for the five of us, counting Felicia—if you want to pick up some French bread and dessert, we'll be set."

"Sounds good." Adelyn opened her notebook and jotted those on the day's listing, then turned to a new page for Maddie's wedding plans.

By the time they finished lunch, Adelyn had half a page of notes, though the conversation had veered into other territory.

Both brides were going to do the bulk of their wedding preparation themselves—especially Maddie since she was on summer break from teaching—but it never hurt to make lists and develop ideas that might help them find whatever would make them happiest. Since Maddie and Ben's pocketbooks were significantly smaller than Reece's, it was handy that the venue would be inexpensive.

Chapter Six

"I might have a client for you." Jason looked up as Adelyn burst into his home, not pausing to say hello before rushing to share her news. "Darla asked me today for a list of contractors who were licensed in town and worked new construction. She and her husband have some land on the edge of town that they want to build on—and she wants a custom home." She set a plastic shopping bag on the counter with something square in the bottom and a loaf of French bread poking out the top.

Excitement hummed in him. "Did you give her my number?"

"Have you filled out your licensing paperwork?" She tipped her head to the side and fluttered her lashes at him.

It was ridiculous that the action would get to him, but he found it adorable—it was so out of character for her, and not actually flirty. How pathetic was he, anyway? "You only sent me the links yesterday—and we spent all evening planting stuff you made me buy on Saturday."

She leaned over and patted him on the cheek. "There, there. I did tell her that you were working on licensing and that you were fabulous. She'll be calling you, but you need to get your paperwork turned in ASAP, along with some examples of your work."

"I can do that. I still need to meet with Charlee and Peter to break the news, but I'm sure that I'll still be working some jobs for them for now."

"I wonder how Peter's dad will feel about it—two new competitors in the past six months, and worse, people who used to work for him."

"I'm an independent subcontractor." Jason knew the distinction would be lost on most people, but he did work for more than Elliot Construction.

"Well, with two weddings in your yard this summer, and a kitchen to finish first, you'll have plenty to do, never mind starting a new business."

"I can do both, it might just take a little longer than I'd like. I'm not exactly a stranger to long hours." He was up in the middle of the night a little too often as well, thanks to his time in Afghanistan. Nighttime maneuvers for so long had messed up his system—not to mention the nightmares he still had a few times per month.

"Well, it's just the yard and this kitchen anyway, right?"

"And the downstairs bathroom, which shouldn't take too long. And the laundry room, but I guess the guests won't see that, so it'll be fine."

"Speaking of your laundry room, I have some great ideas to make it more user friendly. You'll thank me for it." She patted him on the shoulder as she moved past him.

He lifted his brows. "I will?" He had to admit, so far all of her suggestions had been great. She gave his house a homey touch without being frilly, and streamlined every room as they moved through the improvements. "Are you going to reupholster my dining chairs like you did the living room?"

"Sorry, bud, I think they need a good burial more than a fresh coat of paint." She tapped the kitchen island. "This could stay, if you replaced the counter top, stripped the stain and redid it to match whatever cabinets you put in."

"I've been thinking of going industrial–all metal cabinets with mesh baskets and open shelves." He waited for her response, knowing she would hate the idea–it was fun to yank her chain sometimes.

"It's a good thing I know you too well to believe you or I would have to walk out of here right now and never speak to you again. That would be totally wrong for this space and you know it."

"You don't like industrial?"

"Sure I do, in modern houses, not in historic homes with character."

"Can we argue later? We brought dinner." Maddie came through from the living room, her hands full of a Crockpot.

Jason wondered how he had missed sounds of the car pulling in. Adelyn had a way of distracting him like that. "Dinner sounds fantastic."

He high-fived Felicia, slapped Ben's hand and fished some paper plates from the cupboard.

"Where are your real dishes?" Adelyn asked.

"I packed them up to start demolishing this kitchen. That's next on the list after getting the plants in the ground."

"Don't forget the pergola and lattice. They have to be built before we can buy the plants for them." Adelyn was a devil with details.

"I haven't forgotten." But he was starting to second guess this whole wedding in the backyard thing. It was taking on a life of its own. "Man, I could use an extra five sets of hands."

"Well you have four sets tonight, and I'm sure we can find more help for the heavy stuff."

"You know you can count on me when I'm off work," Ben said.

"And I think Tony's looking at getting back to construction work on his off hours."

"Really? He's sick of doing paperwork all day?" Jason asked

"Something like that. He talked about buying a place to fix up, but I don't think he's quite ready to commit."

"Speaking of fixer-uppers," Adelyn asked the happy couple. "Are you going to sell Maddie's place when you get married or rent it out?"

"We'll sell. Work on our homes is one more thing for me to juggle. There are a few more things to upgrade on her place before we can put it on the market."

"For us to juggle," Maddie said, sliding her hand into his. She stared into his eyes and they both smiled. It was kind of sickening, in a nice way. Jason had no idea how that was even possible, but apparently it was. He glanced at Adelyn and saw something pass over her face that looked like longing.

"I'll call Tony then and see what his schedule looks like. You're cutting my summer plans a week short."

"Sorry, we'd do it later, but someone else already took the following weekend." Maddie leaned over and gave her brother a kiss on the cheek. "You are pretty amazing. I appreciate it."

"You just want to save money on the venue. I know your master plan."

"Well, someone convinced both of us to buy houses last year and because of that, we don't have any extra money. You should be glad that's the only thing we're making you do." She shot him a cheeky grin and passed around the plates, since Felicia had already pulled out the bread.

Jason wasn't the only person who was ready to eat.

It didn't take long for them to all settle with a plate full of Crockpot lasagna and bread.

They were nearly finished eating when Maddie shot Jason a look. "When was the last time you went on a date?"

"I date." At least a couple times per year, though he wasn't about to tell her that. It wasn't any of her business. Besides, she knew he wasn't interested in anyone but Adelyn, who sat beside him in complete oblivion.

"Whatever. You should join the online dating site with Adelyn."

Jason's head swiveled toward Adelyn so fast he could swear he popped one of the joints in his spine. "You're on an online dating site?"

"No, but the girls have been pushing. I might give it a whirl. You were right about me needing to look outside the box and consider guys outside of my circle."

"You told her that?" Ben asked. He was also not clueless about Jason's feelings.

"Not exactly." That hadn't been what he'd said—he'd said for her to think outside the box, but that wasn't the same thing as considering guys outside her circle. He had been thinking more of one guy, very much *inside* her circle.

"I think it's a good idea though—I need to meet some new people."

"What's wrong with the old ones?" Jason asked before he could stop himself.

She shook her head as if it should be obvious and changed the subject.

Oh man, what had he done?

"You sure you don't want to create an online profile too?" Adelyn asked Comfrey through the speaker phone. Her hands were busy on the keyboard, filling out the form for KCMeets.com. She had only been home fifteen minutes from planting the last of the bushes at Jason's but decided there was no time like the present.

"No, thank you. I can give you some tips, though. First, don't say you're in Crystal Creek—just focus on the greater KC area."

"But I don't want to meet someone on the other side of the city. I live here."

"Are there that many guys here you don't know who have a prayer of fulfilling your list?"

"There might be. I'm sure there are plenty of moderately ambitious men I wouldn't know because they don't own their own business."

Comfrey chuckled. "Moderately ambitious? Is that what it says on your list?"

"No, but you know, all the guys who have a ton of ambition live to work, rather than working to live. Ambition is important, but so is having a healthy balance in your life. I don't want to be one of those neglected girlfriends."

"Just say that you live in the north-western KC area, then. Besides, maybe he'd be okay with commuting if you got married."

"Okay, I want to get married, but let's focus on a social life first. I won't date guys who couldn't possibly be a prospective husband, but I don't need to rush things."

"You're one of the least rushy people I know. You should try being less deliberate about things and go with the flow once in a while."

"Hey, I can go with the flow." Sometimes. If she knew what to expect.

Maybe she *was* a little too rigid sometimes.

"I'm not saying go totally against your nature—you are who you are—but I know you can be flexible sometimes. Tap into that when you look at guys' profiles. Have fun, give it a chance."

"Have you used a matchmaking service before?"

"I told you I did online dating."

"That's not what I asked." Adelyn wasn't going to let her squeeze out of the discussion if she could help it. "You said real matchmakers exist, even here in the USA, and that they can be really good."

"They can. My sister met her husband through a matchmaker. By all accounts, they're happy. It's not the kind of happiness I'm looking for, too cool and calculated, but it works for them. I have an old sorority friend who used a service too, and she's very happy, in every way, if she's telling the truth."

"Perfectly happy? Is that even possible?" Adelyn doubted it.

"I didn't say perfectly happy, but they have a good marriage, a good friendship, they are still attracted to each other—unless they are very good actors—and she seems as content as anyone I know who met their spouse through the more usual ways."

Adelyn realized Comfrey still hadn't answered her question. Her hands were no longer moving on the keyboard as she focused on the conversation. "Yes, but have *you* tried a service? You keep dodging the question."

There was a long moment of silence before Comfrey responded. "Yes, I used one—or rather, my mom signed me up and tricked me into meeting the matchmaker. I went with it instead of making waves in the middle of the restaurant, plus I was still deep in pleasing-the-parents mode back then. She set me up with a couple guys before one stuck."

"And what happened with him?"

"We dated, things got serious, but in the end, it just couldn't work. Our goals were too different."

Adelyn wondered what Comfry was keeping to herself–her tone said there was more to it than that. "Do you miss him?"

"Sometimes." She sighed. "Okay, a lot, actually. But it is what it is. I can't live the *Huxley way*–I love the life I've built for myself. I don't see Nick moving to a rural area and raising goats."

"Would you use a matchmaker again?"

"The kind of guys who use it all seem to be like my ex–if they're worth dating at all. I don't think that would be a good move for me, though it might work for someone like *you*. If the online dating thing doesn't pan out in a few months, let me know and I'll hook you up."

Adelyn chuckled. Online dating was far enough outside of her comfort zone that she didn't see herself ever going for a matchmaking service, as nice as the benefits might be. "I'll keep that in mind. Industry, hobbies, favorite music," she said as she scanned the list of questions. "I'm surprised they haven't asked what I want to name my future children."

"That would be a handy way to match people up—easier if you both like the same names before you start dating."

Adelyn was surprised at how easy it was to talk to Comfrey. Other than Piper and Maddie, she had never found another woman she could be so open with. "I'm not sure that your favorite baby name is the most important point of compatibility."

"But the children would be less likely to get weird first names."

"Your real name isn't that weird, it's just...very blue blooded." Adelyn saw her business license, so she knew Comfrey's real name, though she had been sworn to secrecy. She didn't get the aversion, personally.

"It's fine for the girl I was trying to be, but it's not fine for who I really am." Comfrey sighed. "I need to be up early tomorrow. I'll catch you later."

"Okay, thanks for recommending the site." Adelyn pushed the button to end the conversation, then focused back on her screen. She was going to give this a real chance, she promised herself that she would. It was past time she moved forward with her life.

Chapter Seven

"There are a lot of business loans and even government grants for women who branch out and start their own businesses." Adelyn stood in front of the group of single women. Many were still living in the women and children's shelter in town, but others had graduated to their own apartments. Classes on bettering their situations continued to be available to those who had left the shelter for as long as they needed them.

Though she knew many of these ladies would never have the drive to branch out on their own, helping them understand the business world could only be good for them. If nothing else, it might help give them a leg up in getting management jobs someday.

A willowy brunette named Natalie, who sat in the back raised her hand. "What kind of laws are there regarding urban farming?"

Adelyn cocked her head. "Honestly, I would have to look that up. I've never had anyone ask me about that before. What exactly are you thinking of when you ask that?"

"Rooftop or urban lot gardens for profit. I've been reading about these small, intensely grown plots where people can actually make a living from a small space—especially in the realm of organic food for restaurants. I wondered if that would be possible here, and if I could add bees or something on the side."

"I know bees are allowed in the city limits, and the law in

Kansas is that you can sell your garden and food products on your own property with minimal paperwork. I'd have to do a little research for specifics. Come into my office sometime—or if you can't during the work day, call me and I'll meet you in the evening if needed. If you have access to space to grow, I'd love to help you make it happen. Comfrey might have more specific information about that than I do, since it's her realm of expertise. I admit, as much as I like to putter in the garden, I'm a long way from being an urban farmer."

She received a few titters at that comment, which wasn't surprising considering how the only time any of them had seen her without her business attire was when she helped in the community garden.

Another woman wanted to start a soap shop, a third dreamed of creating metal sculptures. A fourth wanted to design jewelry. Several others chimed in with their ideas as well.

She had already given them the rundown of what she did for the city. When the questions finally petered out, they ended the meeting and everyone headed for the healthy refreshments Comfrey had provided.

Adelyn handled a couple more questions one-on-one before Comfrey joined her. "I think that went well. We definitely have interest in setting up businesses—this is the largest meeting we've had in a long time."

"I think the Indulgence Row project has helped fuel a lot of interest. It sounds like there's a nice combination of ideas here. It would be great if even half of these women started something new. There's still a long way to go to revive this city." Adelyn studied the ladies as they set food on their plates and talked about possibilities—with a smattering of personal life mixed in.

"I'll have to bring Tony down to talk accounting if interest continues to grow. I'm hoping to cover all kinds of different business-skills topics. If you know of anyone who might have something extra to share, I'd love to add them to the lineup."

Adelyn grinned. "I might know a person or twenty. What kinds of classes did you have in mind?"

"When do you start work on the kitchen?" Tony asked as he poked one end of the 6x6 cedar post into the footing hole.

"As soon as I get the structures up in the yard and everything planted. Adelyn said the plants will need a few weeks to deal with the transplant shock before they take off. It's already getting hot, so I figured I need all the time I can get." Jason stuck his post in the opposite hole while Ben did a third and Reece did the fourth one.

"Are you going to need help with that? I heard you might," Tony said.

"Yeah, if I'm going to finish it up before the wedding, I better get some help. I'm trying to set up my business too, which has turned into a major headache."

"It always does. Let me know if you need any help on the accounting side. I'd be happy to give you a hand either there or with the kitchen."

"Thanks. You want to take a part-time job as an assistant cabinet maker?"

"You're not ordering cabinets?" Reece, who usually dressed up in a suit and tie, wore a dirty white tee and blue jeans, sweat stains, and a grin.

"No, Adelyn and I designed my kitchen for maximum efficiency, and getting custom cabinets would cost way more than my budget. Since I have the skills, and like that sort of thing, I decided to make them myself. It'll take a lot more time, but I'll get exactly what I want for a price I can *almost* afford."

Reece chuckled. "Are you planning to sell her the house when you decide to flip it? She's been giving you a lot of feedback on the design and decoration, hasn't she?"

"I haven't decided if I'm going to sell it yet and, yeah, she's been a big help. Not only with the design, but with some labor as well. I can't complain." Jason didn't want to talk about her, though. He changed the subject back and asked Tony, "Are you thinking of getting out of accounting? I thought you were pretty high up in that company." He grabbed a bag of concrete to set the posts.

"I am, but I don't know. I like accounting well enough, but ten- and twelve-hour days is a little much, even for my love of numbers. I was thinking of opening my own office so I can have a little more control and more free time for other things."

"Like sweating out here in my yard?"

"Hey, it's sunny blistering heat instead of a cool boring office," Tony joked.

"That it is." Jason couldn't imagine giving up construction to go sit in an office all day, even if Reece liked it.

Ben rolled the old wheelbarrow over to them and they mixed concrete for the posts, double-checking them to ensure they were straight up and down and square with each other. Once they had braced the posts, they moved on to the lattice area where the happy couples would stand for their wedding ceremonies. Two of them in August; Holy Hannah, that was a lot of people tromping through his yard. Jason liked people fine, but he also liked to keep his space private.

How did he get talked into hosting the weddings again? Oh yeah, Adelyn asked him to do it.

He focused on his plum line for the lattice post and almost

missed Reece's question to Tony, but his attention was drawn when he heard "bachelor auction."

"What was that?"

"Tony got suckered into being one of Victoria's bachelors for the auction," Ben said with a snicker.

"Hey, it's the autism fundraiser. I figure if a woman wants a date bad enough that she'll make a donation for the kids, then who am I to argue?"

"I'm glad I don't qualify anymore," Reece said. "I know I was on her radar originally. I guess I got back together with Piper just in time."

"No kidding," Ben agreed.

"I'm surprised Adelyn didn't ask you to do it, Jason. I'm sure they could still make a spot for you." Reece shot him a wicked grin.

Jason could swear nothing got past that guy—but then, maybe everyone knew how he felt about Adelyn. Was he that transparent? Did she know? Was that why she mentioned the online dating thing, to discourage him? She hadn't seemed to be making a point. Maybe she was as clueless as she had seemed. He pulled his mind back to the conversation. "She asked. I said no."

"Just no?"

"Straight up not happening. I'm not parading in front of a bunch of screaming women. Or worse, apathetic women."

"Come on, you're a catch. You're turning into an entrepreneur and everything. How could they resist you?" Ben asked, though his voice was mostly teasing.

"Because I've been irresistible up until now. Sorry dude, I have my pride. Even if Tony doesn't."

"Hey! I am proud of who I am, and I can show it off for a good cause. Besides, it's only one date. How bad could it be?"

"Famous last words." Jason shot him a pointed look, then attached the crosspiece to his post.

Chapter Eight

Adelyn would have settled for an hour of listening to fingernails on a chalkboard over another hour of listening to Barry talk about his fishing trips.

This was the reason she didn't accept many first dates. Seriously, what had she been thinking, accepting when he asked her out after a few chats? Granted, it was only dinner at DeQuan's. At least the food was good.

Adelyn smiled and nodded as Barry droned on about his favorite reel. At first she had thought maybe he was nervous, so she had changed the subject a few times, trying to find something else for them to discuss. It did no good—he kept reverting to fishing when she was sure any of the previous subjects would have been sufficient fodder for at least another five minutes of somewhat interesting discussion.

She looked up as the front door opened and saw Jason walk in. She waved him over, not missing the way his brows lifted when he saw who she was with.

"Hi, looks like we had the same idea about dinner," Jason said.

Barry looked at him, as if annoyed at the interruption. "Who are you?"

"He's the older brother of one of my best and oldest friends. Jason, this is Barry. How are things coming in the yard?" Adelyn had helped him the previous night by holding up the lattice while he nailed it in place. Jason and Ben planned to set the rails on the pergola tonight now that the cement had cured enough. She wished she was sweating in his yard right now instead sitting in the air conditioning being bored out of her mind.

"Good, I stopped in for some takeout before we get to work. How do you know each other?" Jason's face was a little stiff as he looked between them, though Adelyn figured Barry wouldn't be able to tell that there was anything wrong.

"Oh, we met online," Barry volunteered. "I meet the most fascinating women online. I love to be able to meet with them for dinner, to get to know them better. Share some good fish stories. There's nothing like a good fish story."

Adelyn was stunned that he thought she was fascinating or that he had any interest in getting to know her, since she had barely gotten a word in for the past forty-five minutes. "Yes, it's been an enlightening conversation. There certainly is nothing like a good fish story." She assumed that was true. She hadn't heard one yet, so she couldn't be sure.

One corner of Jason's mouth twitched upward—no doubt he recognized the utter politeness she employed with people who didn't realize they were being bores.

"Well, you do hear things about those online dating services, but once in a while you get to meet a real peach like Adelyn. You're lucky she agreed to dinner with you, she can be hard to convince."

That was almost mean—the man would think she liked him now, and after dinner, she had every intention of sliding out of here and never talking to him again.

Then Jason made up for it. "Hey, stop by when you get a chance. I have a problem with the laundry room design and I know you can clear it up for me. Tonight, if possible, I have to get everything ordered in the morning." He headed to the front counter where they already had his food ready. He passed over his credit card and was out the door in less than two minutes.

Barry had already returned to another fishing story.

Adelyn glanced at her watch again. Twenty more minutes and she could escape without being rude. Strike one for online dating.

"Laundry room problems?" Adelyn asked when she walked into Jason's backyard half an hour later. "You already ordered everything for the laundry room, and the design wasn't that complicated."

"Well, maybe not so much. Mostly I wanted to give you a reason to get out if you needed to. You didn't look fascinated by his conversation."

"I love conversation, it can often be fascinating. But you're right, his was not—a conversation, I mean—I barely got a word in between stories of his fishing trips."

"Not a great date?" Tony grinned. "If you had agreed to go out with me, we would have had fun."

"That was ten years ago and I already had a date for the dance. You're not still pining over little ol' me, are you?" She fluttered her lashes outrageously.

"Honey, I don't think anyone could get over loving you. You believe me, don't you?"

"Not even a little bit. Looks like you're making good headway—you must have zoomed through your Chinese food."

"Jason is a slave driver, and eats as fast as a hungry orphan," Tony acceded to the change in topic, with no more reaction than if she had said she preferred orange chicken to sweet and sour.

Jason ignored the jab and grabbed two more boards to set across the largest planks.

"It was my first foray into online dating. Not the best experience, but it'll get better. Right?"

"Sure, you keep telling yourself that." Tony grabbed his end and set the board in the pre-cut groove.

"You're not making me feel better."

"Sorry, I'm a little distracted here. He said you were the one hounding him about getting this done."

"She is. The to-do list for this yard and the house before the weddings seems to grow every day," Jason lifted the cordless drill and pre-drilled a hole into the long support beam.

"I'm saving you headaches in July when your sister will be hounding you night and day if it's not done. Besides, my sparkling personality makes up for my pushiness."

Jason shot her a dry look but didn't argue, which was good enough for her.

Content that she wasn't needed and that the pergola would be done before dark, Adelyn headed for the pathway they had been preparing for flagstone. Garden beds lay on either side, mostly empty with a few new plants dotting them and a handful of weeds breaking through the soil. She took a moment to pull the weeds as she walked by, enjoying the relative peace of the yard, despite the noise of the electric drill in the background. This was a place of peace, a place where she could sit back and release the day's pressure. That was part of what she had been trying to create with Comfrey when they designed the yard. She hoped it would appeal to anyone who bought the house, if he sold it.

Maybe she should buy it.

The thought hadn't occurred to her before. It was much too large for a single person—which was why she figured he would sell. If it was too big for a single guy, it was definitely too big for just her. Maybe she should think of a smaller design, something also in the

Victorian vein, and a cozy backyard. He could build it for her, and she would have fun designing the layout.

Adelyn had a nice chunk of cash for a down payment. She should start thinking about where she wanted to land eventually—somewhere more permanent than the condo she currently rented.

She circled back around to the pergola. They had quite a bit more shopping to do for annuals and some flowering perennials. The paths needed to be laid, and the pond installed. She thought helping Jason build the garden might be just what she needed to unwind on days when the community garden didn't need attention.

Her phone buzzed and she got a PM from Barry.

Had a good time. You want to get dinner again sometime. Maybe tomorrow, at my house?

Nope, not happening. Maybe she should have been less polite about her feelings before she left that night. *That's very sweet of you, but I'm pretty busy for the next couple weeks.*

Adelyn looked around again. This place could provide adequate excuses for brushing guys off for quite a while.

Jason and Tony were setting the last board into place when he looked up and met her gaze. A smile flashed over his angular face and she smiled back. A night with Jason was far more interesting than with most other guys.

And at least she wouldn't have to listen to fish tales.

Chapter Nine

Getting dressed up for a night out had always been one of life's small pleasures. Though Adelyn didn't have a date for the bachelor auction—it would be weird to go with a date to something like that, even if she weren't there as a volunteer—she enjoyed the ritual anyway. It had always been her favorite part of the social events her mother would take her to when she was growing up. Not that she minded an occasional visit into the society her mother loved, but it wasn't where Adelyn wanted to spend the majority of her time.

She was pulling in front of the building when her phone started to ring. Jason's name popped up on the car display or she would have let it go to voicemail—she was running behind. "Hello?"

"Hi, I had some questions about the kitchen plans. Could you swing by to look them over? Or I could pop over there if you'd rather," Jason asked.

"I can stop to look at them tomorrow." They had been going back and forth over some details on the island, though why he didn't just make the final decision, she didn't know—it was his house.

"Not tonight?"

"No, I'm headed to the bachelor auction right now. I'll swing by tomorrow afternoon, though, to check them out." She saw an empty space in the back of the lot and cursed herself for arriving later than she had planned.

There was a half a moment's pause. "The bachelor auction? Are you planning to put up some money on Tony?"

"Don't be silly, if I wanted to date Tony, I'd ask him out. I just arrived and need to go. I'll talk to you tomorrow." She hung up the phone using the button on her steering wheel, and slid into the open spot. She hated running behind. Victoria wanted the helpers to be there promptly at six to help collect entrance fees and give directions. They managed to get twenty very eligible bachelors to agree to participate and had pre-sold two to three times as many tickets for the women. Everyone would enjoy a—hopefully—delicious dinner in addition to the bidding. There was also a silent auction on the side with dating activities that people could buy either for themselves or for their potential date with one of the bachelors. Area businesses had been very generous in providing the auction items—Adelyn was tempted to bid for a couple of them herself.

Victoria put Adelyn right to work, setting out the silent auction items and bid sheets. She was surprised to see that there were tables for far more than the eighty people she had expected. Next time Victoria rushed by, Adelyn snagged her.

"How many tickets did we sell?"

Victoria leaned in, glee on her face. "A hundred and twenty—at double the cost of the dinner. And we haven't even started the auctions yet."

"That is fantastic. I can't believe it." She knew it was for a great cause and was thrilled to be part of it, however small her role might be.

Several of the bachelors showed up—she was familiar with most of them, at least by reputation if not in person, and made small talk as she led them back to where they would wait for the night to start.

She didn't get a chance to talk to Tony when he arrived, but they waved from across the room and she swapped smiles with Matthew Craig.

The room started to fill up and Adelyn greeted guests, taking tickets and directing them to their seats. She recognized some of the faces, but many were new to her—and surprisingly, there were many couples in the crowd who had apparently come for the entertainment, or to have their faces appear in the right circles. Most surprising of all, though, was to see Comfrey come up the hall toward her.

Adelyn almost didn't recognize her, Comfrey wore something clingy and elastic in a rich red that scooped wide enough to show off her collar bones, but with an otherwise demure neckline and an ankle-teasing length. It was modest but came across as daring, which must have been the results of a top-notch designer. Comfrey had her hair in a sleek up-do and tendrils curled around her face and along her neck, the bleached blond and dyed black of her hair twining together artfully. Her makeup was much darker and more dramatic than Adelyn had ever seen.

Adelyn whistled. "You look amazing. I guess I shouldn't be surprised, but I don't think I've ever even seen you in a skirt, never mind formal wear."

"Thanks, you're not so bad yourself. I love your dress."

Adelyn was fond of the blue sheath, though it wasn't nearly as fancy as most of the dresses other people wore. "I didn't expect you here tonight."

"Every six or eight months I dress up in something fancy and go to an event so I can send my mom pictures, reassuring her that I am still involved with *the right kind of people*." She rolled her eyes as she said this. "The ticket was ridiculous, but it's going to a good cause and I know Victoria said the hotel is giving them a break on the food. How can I resist?"

"Well, I hope you enjoy the dinner and the entertainment. And check out the silent auction—there are some great items up for bid."

"What more does a girl need than a spa day or two?" Comfrey asked as she entered the main room.

Adelyn believed that Comfrey meant that with no intention to bid on a bachelor for herself—until she put in a last-minute bid for Tony. Six-hundred dollars was a hefty price for dinner with someone you could have asked out any day of the week. Not that it had been the largest amount bid—at a thousand dollars, Mari's bid for Tyler Jackson easily outstripped everyone else.

Adelyn didn't get a chance to talk to Comfrey before she and Tony each left for the night, but she vowed to herself that she would catch up with the other woman soon.

By the time she finished helping Victoria clean up after the guests had gone for the night, Adelyn was exhausted, but very pleased with their accomplishment. The charity had fared better than any year on record, coming in at twenty--thousand dollars.

"What was the big rush?" Adelyn asked when she dropped by Jason's place the next afternoon. It had been late when she finished up at the auction and even later by the time she removed her finery and makeup, changing into pajamas for the night. After being up late, church had started way too early.

"I guess it wasn't a rush," he said as he let her in. "I thought about how I work in the kitchen and wondered what you thought about switching a few things." He led her to the dining table and flipped open the folder where he kept a printout of the plans they had been refining.

"Okay, well, it's your house, so if you think it should be different, then you should change it." She slid into the chair beside the folder, though, so he could show her what he had in mind.

"Of course, but I wanted to make sure I wasn't forgetting the reason you suggested the other way." He pulled out a sheet of vellum he had used to draw the plan variation. "I was thinking about the suggestions you made for the laundry area and it made me think." He explained the rearrangement and grabbed the yellow notebook to sketch out the shelf plan he was thinking of.

Adelyn stared at him for a moment, stunned that she hadn't thought of it.

"What, is it a stupid idea?"

"No, it's brilliant. I love it. It's almost perfect. What if we combined the two?"

She took the offered pencil and added a few lines to the draft. She couldn't help notice the warmth of his shoulder, which pressed lightly against hers as he leaned in to see her work. Nor did she miss the spicy scent of his cologne which faintly drifted over to her—just strong enough to enjoy without being overpowering.

"That's great. Thanks," he said when he saw the adjustments she suggested. "I'll re-draw those and figure out the supplies so I can order everything."

"Good. Your kitchen is going to be amazing. If you're planning to sell when you finish the house, having the weddings here will be great advertisement to spread the word." If she didn't decide to buy it herself, anyway.

"You think I should sell?" Jason asked.

She shrugged. "It seems pretty big for one person, but I love the house. I was thinking how much I would love to live somewhere like this, but realistically, if I were going to build something for me, I'd have to pick something smaller."

"Are you thinking of building? Because I know someone who does new construction." Jason grinned at her.

She chuckled. "I happen to know everyone with a construction license in town, but I'll keep you in mind if I need a recommendation."

"I only have one recommendation. And I would be totally offended if you didn't take it."

"I couldn't risk offending you." She yawned, thinking she could use a Sunday afternoon nap.

"Did you have a late night with your date?" Jason asked.

"It was late, but I told you I was at the auction."

"Yes, you did. Who did you bid on?"

"No one. I was there as a volunteer. Didn't I say that?" She thought back on their conversations about the auction, but couldn't remember if she had told him what she was doing there.

His shoulders seemed to relax slightly. "No, you didn't. How did it go?"

"Great, really great. We raised a bundle of money for the charity and you'll never believe who bought an evening with Tony."

"Layla Jennings?" He referred to Reece's ex who had caused trouble for Reece and Piper when they got back together the previous winter.

"No, but just as bad—Tiffany Trainer. I haven't seen her since that incident in Chili's. *Comfrey* bid on him."

Jason's forehead wrinkled. "But she could ask him out anytime. Why spend a bunch of cash for a date?"

"The charity, I guess. Or to save him from a night of misery. I was surprised to see her there, all decked out in something slinky. She said she does it to send pictures to her mom to prove she's getting out in the *right kind of crowd*."

"The right kind of crowd?"

"Her parents are very focused on their social lives." Adelyn understood. Her parents weren't quite as focused on their image as many of their friends, but there was still pressure to put in appearances.

"Sometimes I look at people and their kids and have to shake my head. I have no idea how high society produced someone like Comfrey."

"It sure shows how much influence our natures can have compared to our upbringing."

"Yeah. So, what did you do at the auction? Don't tell me you weren't tempted to bid on anyone."

"Maybe one or two, but the opening bid was more than I was willing to pay for a date with a stranger. I did put my name on a couple packages for the silent auction, but was outbid on them as well. That was fine, I was there to help, not to spend money."

"Too bad on the silent auction. I'll have to ask Tony how it went for him."

Wishing she could go home for a nap, Adelyn checked her watch. "I probably ought to get to dinner with my mom and Clark. I'm sure your parents are expecting you, too."

"Mom would shoot me if I missed."

"I heard Angelina was coming home for the weekend."

"Yeah, we heard the same rumor, but she called and made excuses on Friday, hours after she should have already been on her way. Mom was not happy about it."

Adelyn could understand why. The youngest McCormick had all but disappeared when she moved to New York City, determined to make it big on Broadway. "What's going on with her?" Adelyn didn't get it. She had struggles with her family, but seven years without coming home to visit was excessive.

"I don't know. I wish I did. She's talked about being involved with big shows on Broadway, but she's never sent pictures or playbills."

"Maybe if she's not going to come home, you guys should visit her instead."

"I've been thinking that too. She's promised to come home for Maddie's wedding. We'll have to see."

Adelyn had been nudging Maddie to visit Angelina as well, but other than their parents, who had flown out to see their daughter a few times, no one else had gone. Adelyn couldn't figure out why—if there had been a big rift, she would have heard about it.

She left Jason's a few minutes later, and after checking her hair and lipstick in the mirror, headed to her mom's house.

The place where Michele and Clark lived was a large mini-mansion in the same part of town as Reece, though their subdivision was several years older.

It was a nice place in a quiet neighborhood with quarter-acre lots and plenty of trees for privacy. The two-story structure sat back on the lot with a big circular drive out front and a four-car garage eating up the acreage around the side. Adelyn parked on the circular drive and walked up the front steps. She could put on a happy face for her mom and get along for a couple hours.

Chapter Ten

Adelyn saw the notification of a new comment in her KCMeets app while she was in the middle of the Monday managers' meeting. Things had gone so spectacularly badly in that first face-to-face date that she had been unsure about meeting anyone else. She flipped her phone over so she wouldn't see any other notifications come through and finished the meeting.

In no hurry to see yet another message from some guy just looking to hookup for the night or to fend off someone twice her age, she ignored the notification that now said she had three messages as she typed up her notes from the meeting, handled incoming email and voicemail messages, and contacted someone about the morning's discussion.

It was lunch before Adelyn sat back in her office chair and looked at her messages. She was up to four now. Three of them she deleted after reading because the guys were crass and obviously looking for only one thing—and that was one thing that she wasn't looking for—maybe she should make a note of that in her profile? Was there something there that made the other guys on the site think she was only after sex and not a relationship?

Before reading the fourth message, she scrolled back through her profile and changed up the wording, though she didn't think there was anything questionable to begin with. Then she flipped back to the final message.

Royalsfan126—that was not very creative. She read the message though, and was instantly intrigued.

Hi, I know these things are supposed to be mostly anonymous, but I've seen you in the bank a few times. I'm a loan officer there, with a focus on small businesses and couldn't help but notice you. Honestly, I thought about asking you out, but I didn't think I would have a chance, so I never did. Once I saw you here, I thought maybe we could at least see if we have anything in common, and then maybe I'd get up the guts to ask you for dinner. Don't worry, I won't stalk you at the city offices if you say no.

A few things about me: I'm a single dad—my wife died in a car accident a few years ago, so it's just me and my four-year-old son. I've been working at State Bank of Crystal Creek for five years—basically since I finished my loan officer's certification. I grew up in Tonganoxie so we didn't go to school together, though unless you hate football, we probably attended some games together—Alexa Meyers works with me and said you grew up here. You went to school together, right? Anyway, I'm not looking for a one-night stand, I'm looking for a relationship, which is what your profile said you want as well. Okay, I need to send this before I lose my nerve. Again. I hope to hear back from you. Daniel

Adelyn stared at the paragraph—it was clearly not scripted or polished, but she was more impressed than with any of the other first-contact messages she'd gotten so far. And hey, someone did manage to notice she was looking for an actual relationship. The fact that he lived locally was a big bonus, and he had a nice face. Dark hair, brown eyes, and a smile that brightened his whole expression. If she had seen him when she was in the bank, she hadn't noticed him, and she wondered why not. Was she too self-absorbed to notice people around her?

She thought she could like this guy. Sucking in a breath, Adelyn hit reply. *Hi, Daniel, it's good to meet you, and a relief, really, to* *find someone who seems like a real human instead of a put-on shell looking for a hookup. Yes, I grew up here. I had big plans for what I would do with my life after college, but the fact was, I wanted to be home again—not home at my parents' place necessarily, but back in Crystal Creek. When the position opened up at the city, I jumped at the chance to switch from my job in Lawrence to come back here. I don't know if I can be friends with someone from Tonganoxie though, you were our bitterest enemies—though I understand *your* biggest rival was a different school. (Isn't it funny how little that even matters now?) I think I'd like to get to know you a little better. And maybe even grab dinner if things go well online. I'm a big fan of dinner.*

She hit send before she could second-guess, then scribbled a note in her planner to catch up with Alexa and find out more about Daniel. Since his son was still preschool aged, she wouldn't be able to get Maddie to glean information about him through the elementary school teacher grapevine.

Feeling more optimistic on the dating front than she had in a long time, she stood from her chair and headed out for a quick lunch. She had spent half her break dealing with KCMeets, but maybe she would get lucky and have a reason to stop using the site at the end of the month. That thought made her smile all the brighter.

Four days after Adelyn met Daniel online, and about thirty exchanges later, she stood in the vestibule at Brisket and Noodles, waiting for him to arrive. She had gotten there early tonight, wanting a moment to double-check her appearance after her arrival, due to the pounding rain outside. Now she watched through the window as cars pulled into the parking lot, watching the people pull out their umbrellas for the trip into the restaurant, or make a dash for it without protection, making it inside with hair that was more than a little damp.

A little blue Honda parked in the lot and she watched and waited. There was a dark-haired man inside, but she couldn't see his face. She saw him paw through something beside him before turning to open the door and launching an umbrella upward.

She laughed when she saw what he carried—the canopy was covered in teenage Mutant Ninja Turtles. When he turned fully toward the door, she recognized him from his picture—and the one on the bank website, which she had looked up before agreeing to a date. She had also checked up on him with Alexa—he'd gotten good marks from someone Adelyn had known for years. After a little waffling, she had decided to give him a chance.

Daniel looked at his watch and pursed his lips. Adelyn glanced at her wrist as well and realized he was a few minutes late—not enough to count as a mark against him in her book, though.

He entered the restaurant, pushing through the heavy door and his eyes immediately fell on her. "Adelyn?"

"That's me." She slid her hand into his and shook it. He had a good grip, firm, but not too tight.

"I'm sorry I'm a little late. I got sucked into a phone call with a client."

"No problem, it happens to all of us."

The hostess checked to see if they were ready to be seated, and then led them into the dining area.

A moment later they were seated at a corner booth with a great view of the rainy parking lot. The storm seemed to increase in ferocity as they were seated and Adelyn was glad they were both already inside. They talked about their families—she gave him an abridged version of her parents' many marriages—their education, and he talked a little about his son. Daniel was nice, seemed pretty open, and he made her laugh. These were all things she liked, so she let herself relax as they lingered over dinner and dessert.

"So you work with small business loans. How long have you been doing that?" She'd been wanting to ask all night, but wanted to get a little more familiar with him first.

"Two years with small business. I started in home loans, which is good work, but I like working with entrepreneurs and seeing them go for their dreams. It may not be the most exciting job, but it works for me and I'm good with numbers."

That brought her around to the topic she wanted to discuss most. "I imagine there are a lot of loan and grant programs out there for single women, especially single mothers, who are looking to start their own businesses, aren't there?"

"A lot. I've helped several people apply for grants in conjunction with the loans for start-up capital. Why, are you looking to branch out on your own?" He reached across the table and ran his fingers over hers.

Enjoying the casual contact, Adelyn laughed at the thought. "No, not at all. I love my job. I work with a women's and children's shelter. They offer weekly classes to help current and former residents get back on their feet and learn different skills. A couple weeks ago I talked to a group of them about my job working with businesses in the area and it sounded like a number of them were thinking of starting their own businesses. I think a couple already have, on a very small scale. They might be interested in a presentation specifically about financing a new business, if you'd agree to teach it." Now that she had asked the question, she hoped she wasn't stepping outside her bounds—a few presentations and helping the women set up their garden beds in the community garden did not make her an expert, and she wasn't exactly in charge of arranging these presentations, but she figured Comfrey would be happy to schedule one.

"I think it's a great idea. Give whoever is in charge my contact information and tell them I'd love to help if they need me." Daniel fished out a business card and handed it to her.

"Great. I'll do that." Adelyn elaborated a little more on some of the other classes they had offered and what some of the women who had graduated from the program were doing with their lives now. She had only been involved with them peripherally, and mostly just since she and Comfrey had become friends, but it had been a great experience, giving back in that way.

Finally Daniel looked at his watch. "I probably ought to get home—I have a babysitter, but I try to be home for the bedtime routine myself, especially since I've been at work all day."

"It was good to meet you, officially," Adelyn said.

He took her hand, drawing her gaze up to his. "I'd love to do this again sometime."

"I'd like that too." She was glad he'd asked, and had actually been nervous that he wouldn't, that he would be glad to have the night over with, though she couldn't figure out why she was worried about it.

Since he had already paid for dinner, they stood, taking the cartons of leftovers, and he led her outside. The rain had stopped at some point during their date and though the ground still had plenty of puddles, there were already a few dry patches. They said goodnight and separated at his car—she crossed a few stalls over to hers and got inside. He waited until she backed out of the parking stall, then waved and preceded her out of the parking lot.

Had he waited to make sure her car would start and she didn't have any trouble? What a nice guy.

When she got to the first red light, she glanced at her messages.

There was one from Jason. *You on for tomorrow morning at 8? There's a lot to do.*

You betcha. She wrote back. The lattice and pergola were both finished, and they had gotten a bunch of prep work out of the way that week, so they were ready to plant the rest of the flowers and vines. She couldn't wait to see the final result.

Chapter Eleven

The summer heat was frying Jason's brain, he was sure of it. Otherwise, how could he find a sweaty, disheveled Adelyn so darn appealing? He had hit the nursery to pick up the last of the plants first thing this morning and been back home with the items she had picked out days earlier before she showed up at eight, looking fresh and adorable in a bold pink blouse and blue shorts. The others had arrived shortly after her, looking somewhat less well put together than Adelyn—but then, she was almost always the most fashionable of the group in any setting. The ground was soft and damp after the heavy rains the evening before, so planting went quickly.

Adelyn was happy, bright, and laughing constantly, which pleased him, until Maddie's question half an hour after they started illuminated why.

"How did the date go last night?" Maddie asked her.

"Great, really great, actually. It was probably the best first date I've ever had."

Jason turned his head slowly, not wanting to appear as anxious as he suddenly felt. "You had a date last night? Not with one of those weirdos from the dating website."

"Yes, I did meet him online, but no, not one of the weirdos—he's a super nice guy. He's a single father and works as a loan officer at a bank here in town."

"Which means his paycheck varies a lot," Jason pointed out. "That can be pretty unstable."

"Not at all like construction, then?" She arched a brow at him.

He wished he had held his tongue. "It's not totally feast or famine in my business." More like regular food or famine, but no need to point that out.

Her brows lifted at him in puzzlement before she turned back to Maddie. "He was nice, thoughtful, tipped well, and talked about his son several times."

"He's married?"

"A widower. He was left with an infant and had to figure out the parenting thing on his own. I'm impressed with that."

No, no. This could not be happening. She was supposed to go for Jason, the guy standing in front of her. The guy who knew her better than anyone else out there—well, any male out there, anyway. What was she doing dating someone else? He had just started making headway on her list.

"Are you going to see him again?" Comfrey asked, oblivious to the dagger she was digging into his chest with every question.

"Yeah. Oh, and he said he'd be happy to present on business loans and grants at the women's group."

"Perfect. There was definitely interest in the subject after you talked to them."

Apparently the unnamed man was a saint. Jason hated him even more for that—as if he needed more reason to hate any guy Adelyn dated. He sucked in a breath and turned away to get the last two pots. It would be fine—it had been one date. Surely her list would kick in and she would realize the guy had a fatal flaw. In the meantime, he was going to be there, putting check marks next to every item on her list.

"You're taking the news of her dating calmly," Ben muttered to

Jason when they knelt to add the clematis vine to the north-east corner of the pergola.

"There's no point in getting upset." Even if he was. "It's a first date, not a lifetime commitment. I have a plan. I'll just follow the plan."

He hoped that would be enough.

"I wanted to thank you for all of your help with the yard," Jason said. He was getting good at calling when she was running out the door to something.

Adelyn shifted her cell phone to fit between her ear and shoulder better as she finished packing her purse for the evening. She had another date with Daniel in ten minutes. The weather was nice and they talked about getting a pizza and going to the park with his son. "You know I helped because it's my two best friends getting married, right?" she asked. "If anything, I should be thanking you for being open to my ideas for the yard and going along with the craziness they produced."

"My neighbors thank you for it too," he continued, as if she hadn't spoken. "They're much happier with the new landscaping than the mess that was my yard last summer."

"You're welcome." She checked to make sure she had the right lipstick and glanced in the mirror to see if she still looked okay.

"I wanted to take you for some dinner and an activity that is not garden-related to say thanks."

"Um sure, whenever is probably fine." She flipped open her planner and double-checked the events in the next week, which included the Fourth of July madness. "How about Friday?" She realized her earrings didn't go with her current outfit and headed to the closet to pick out new ones.

"Are you in the middle of something?" Jason asked. "You seem distracted."

"Yeah, sorry, I'm getting ready to leave, so I'm a little scatterbrained." She picked out a pair of small gold hoops and removed the larger blue dangles that had matched her work outfit. "Does Friday work for you?"

"Yeah, that would be fine. Do you have another first date tonight?"

"No, second date with Daniel and Ralphie."

"Wait, Ralphie? Who's Ralphie?"

"Oh, Daniel's son. We're all having pizza in the park—practically a perfect combination on a day like today."

"Right. Well, Friday, dress casual—like jeans casual, not office casual. And come hungry. I'll pick you up at six."

"Okay, sure. Have you finished the paperwork for your business license?" She hadn't heard anything for a few days.

"Everything is filed with the state. I just need to take my test and then I can apply for my city business license."

"Good. Darla was going to call you. Did she?" One earring in. She shifted the phone to the other side while she fumbled with the second one.

"Yeah, I'm meeting with them tomorrow to look at their house plans and get a feel for their expectations."

"Oh good. She's so easy-going. I don't know her husband very well, but I think they'll be a great couple to work with." Adelyn turned to the full-length mirror and checked her appearance, and was pleased with the result.

"Right. Well, have fun on your date."

"I will." She got back to her planner and jotted in the time and other info. "See you then. Gotta go, bye!"

"Goodbye."

Adelyn adjusted her watch, then slid her planner back into her purse and retrieved her keys. Time to go.

It wasn't until she was nearly to the park that she realized Jason had asked her on what might be construed as a date. She shook her head. "Of course it's not a date—it's only a thank-you dinner and activity." They'd done things like that before and it hadn't meant anything. There was no reason to think it would mean something now.

She put it out of her head—time to focus on the real date. And the very real guy sitting at a picnic table near the playground with a very large pizza box sitting closed in front of him.

Daniel was dressed down in jeans and a tee instead of the white button-down shirt and dress pants he had worn when coming straight from work the previous date. She was glad she had changed into something more casual before meeting with him.

A dark-haired little boy called out to Daniel from the top of the slide as Adelyn locked her car doors behind her. Daniel called back and the boy slid down the bumpy green slide, grinning from ear to ear.

"Good job, Ralphie! Was it fun?"

"Yeah! Can I have pizza now?"

"I think that's a great idea," Adelyn agreed.

Daniel turned toward her and smiled. "Good, I wouldn't want it to get cold." He waved his son back to the table and made the introductions. "Ralphie, this is Miss Adelyn. She's joining us for dinner."

"Why?" Ralphie asked.

"Because I'm hungry." Adelyn wasn't sure what his father wanted him to know about his dating life, so she decided to keep it as casual as possible until they could work out their dynamics.

Ralphie looked her over, then nodded his approval. "Okay. Do you like pineapple on your pizza? Dad likes pineapple, but I think it's yucky."

"Me too. But that's okay, we can always pull it off, right?"

He nodded decisively. He slid in across from his father, who handed him a wet wipe. "Wash your hands with this."

Ralphie scrubbed it over his hands and passed it back so Daniel could tuck it away in a bag. "I try not to be too crazy about germs, but dirt is dirt. I got half Hawaiian, and half pepperoni—which is the only kind Ralphie likes."

"That's because he's obviously very smart." She accepted the plate of pizza Daniel handed her and the three of them talked while they ate. Okay, Ralphie talked non-stop for ten minutes, having to be reminded to eat something repeatedly, while Adelyn and Daniel nodded their heads and made short sentences of agreement between bites. She was famished—lunch seemed like it was days behind her instead of only six hours.

After Daniel had removed traces of sauce from Ralphie's hands and face with another wipe, he sent the boy back to the playground to swing.

"Dinner's not exactly a good opportunity for conversation when he's around," he said.

"It's not a problem. He's adorable—and funny."

"Watching him crack himself up is funnier than what he actually says."

"True. I love seeing kids with a healthy ability to entertain themselves."

"That's very kind of you. You were good with him."

"It must have been difficult, raising him alone, especially when he was tiny and needed so much attention." She admired that about him when so many fathers seemed to take a more passive role—including her own.

"No more difficult than for other people. Less difficult than for many, I'd guess. At least I make enough to afford good daycare. It's harder finding good care, honestly. He's, um, very lively, and some of the sitters I've used haven't been prepared to deal with that on top of the kids they already had."

"How long were you married?" Adelyn knew this probably wasn't second-date fodder, but she wanted to know.

"A little over two years. We were married a little under a year when she got pregnant. Ralphie was six months old when she was in the accident."

"Wow. Was he in the car with her?"

"No, she was heading to a girl's night with her sister. She was the only one in the car, thankfully." He looked over the gravel to his son. "I can't imagine if I had lost them both."

Ralphie climbed into the swing and waved them over. "Come push me."

Adelyn grinned. "Looks like we're being summoned.

They joined Ralphie and Adelyn took the swing beside him. Daniel pushed them both until it was time to get his son home for the night and into bed.

As they walked back to the cars, Daniel asked, "One of my coworkers is having a barbecue Friday night. Would you like to join me?"

"That sounds fun, but I have dinner plans that night. I wish I could."

"Dating several guys?"

"No, I'm only dating you." Adelyn remembered her question about whether or not Jason thought it was a date. "He's an old friend. I helped him with a project in his yard and he's saying thanks. I could see about rescheduling."

"No, that's okay. I'll try again another time. What about lunch Saturday?"

She shook her head. "Jason's sister Maddie is getting married—in his yard, which is why I needed to do some yard work. Anyway, the girls are getting together to go dress shopping Saturday."

"When do you have an opening?"

Adelyn reached into her car and pulled out her notebook. She flipped it open to the coming week.

"Wow, what is that?"

"It's a bullet journal. Part planner, part journal, part brain-dump central. It literally tracks everything in my life." She flipped through and pointed out wedding lists for her friends, birthday lists, daily planning pages and a cleaning list for her apartment.

"Wow, that's got some serious color going on."

She pulled out one of the multi-color pens from the strap on back of her notebook. "All the better to keep everything straight."

"You don't use an electronic calendar?"

"I do for work, but I like the tactile feel of paper. How does Wednesday look for you?"

He consulted the calendar on his phone. "We have a T-ball game."

"Thursday night?"

"My babysitter has a class then and Saturday is out. What about lunch on Sunday, you could come to my place and we'll have something from the grill, and some sides from the grocery store so they'll be edible."

"That sounds great."

"Is there anything you don't or can't eat?" he asked.

"I'm pretty easy to please. Can I bring something? Maybe dessert?"

"Sure, if you want to." He took her notebook and wrote his address in under the Sunday heading. "Now you won't lose it."

"Perfect." Adelyn looked up and he was only inches away, his gaze tight on hers.

"I've had a good time with you. Thanks for agreeing to come out with me."

"Ditto." She thought for a moment that he was going to kiss her, but then Ralphie tugged on his pants and whined to go home.

Daniel brushed his lips across her cheek and whispered in a low, throaty voice, "I can't wait."

Adelyn smiled as they walked away. She slid into her car and tucked her planner back into her purse. Oh yeah. He might be the one.

Chapter Twelve

Adelyn hadn't known what to expect when Jason had cryptically told her to be ready to go as soon as the office closed, and to wear pants that day and bring a hair elastic. Seriously, what did he have planned, and why wouldn't he tell her?

Still, she hadn't protested too loudly—he promised an experience she wouldn't forget, and she trusted him. She always had.

The fact that he was willing to cut out of work a little early to clean up and pick her up, plus take an evening away from the other things he had to do at home that she knew were putting pressure on him, made her even more willing to give him some leeway.

She wasn't surprised when Jason walked into her office two minutes before the outside doors would be locked for the night. He tended to be punctual. And man did he look fine in those perfectly snug jeans and Royals t-shirt. His short, dark hair was still slightly damp from the shower and the thin strip of beard that followed along his jawline and across the bottom of his chin looked freshly trimmed. "Hey, you about ready?" he asked when he came to stop at her door.

She managed not to check the corner of her mouth for drool as she smiled back at him. "Sure. Just let me shut this down." She closed her email program and logged off her computer for the night. "How was work?"

"Pretty good. Only a few minor snags, easily worked out. How about you?"

"I've been talking to Victoria about some new businesses coming into the Indulgence Row rehab. It's going to be fun. Is this outfit okay?" She stood and moved out from behind the desk. She had opted for a simple blouse, dress pants, and sensible flats rather than the skirt and heels she often wore.

He looked at her footwear. "You'll probably be more comfortable in sneakers, but those will do in a pinch."

"I have something a little more comfortable in the car, but we can swing by my place for hiking boots if that's what you had in mind." Please, no. If she changed to boots, she would have to change into some jeans, and switch socks. And then she would have to suffer him poking at her for being a fashion snob—she wasn't, she just liked to look put together when she was in public and hiking boots definitely did not work with dress pants. She swung her purse onto her shoulder and checked it for her keys, then snagged her omnipresent water bottle.

"I don't think hiking boots are necessary. We'll take a look at what you have in the car. But like I said, those shoes would probably work in a pinch." He shifted to let her go through her office door first, then followed behind, waiting while she locked the door for the night.

She poked her head into a couple offices to say goodnight to her coworkers, and stepped into the blast of hot Kansas air. Ninety-five degrees with seventy-percent humidity led to a heat index above one-hundred. She honestly had no clue how road and construction crews managed being outside all day every day.

She stopped by her car and pulled out the other shoes—they

were still somewhat dressy to coordinate with her outfit, but had a better sole and padding in case they were going to be on their feet.

"Looks good. We won't be doing a ton of walking, though."

"What are we doing?"

"Well, first, we're going to have a snack, because we need to get to Overland Park before six, and then we'll have a real dinner after."

"After what?"

"After the activity." He shot her a grin, obviously enjoying keeping her in the dark.

"You aren't going to tell me, are you?"

"That's why it's called a surprise."

"But–" She stopped talking when his finger came within half an inch of her lips, silencing her. She looked up into his hazel eyes and felt her chest clutch.

Something passed between them for a few seconds as they stared at each other, and when he spoke, his voice was low. "I double-checked with Maddie before I made the plans, to make sure you would be okay with this and she agreed with me that it would be fun and you'd like it, so stop worrying about it."

How could she argue with that? She nodded, and wondered for a moment what it would feel like to have that long finger caress along her upper lip, then took a step back. She'd had a crush on him once and got over it. She didn't need to do it again. No way was she going there. "Okay, I trust you."

"No, you trust Maddie, but I'll take it." He waited while she sat on her driver's seat and changed shoes, setting the ones she'd worn all day onto the floor in front of the passenger seat, then relocked her door, sliding the keys back into her purse.

They headed into the city, turning down I-35 toward the I-435 interchange. "You said something about snacks?" Adelyn asked after they were out of Crystal Creek. She had anticipated eating first and her lunch had been hurried between projects so she could be sure to get out of the office on time for once.

"Right." He pointed to the small cooler he used for his lunches, which sat on the floor between them. "I picked up a variety, though I figured you would go for the eclair."

Adelyn flipped open the lid and peered into the cooler. She should have known he would choose wisely. In it was half a dozen assorted pastries from donuts to Danishes and her beloved eclairs. She chose the chocolate-covered beauty and took a bite of the soft flaky crust. "You sure know how to show a girl a good time. Don't you love, well, everything Sweet Confections makes?"

"It's the best. Maybe not as good as your caramel sweet rolls, but still really great."

She grinned. That recipe did happen to be one of the best on the planet.

The drive zoomed past as they talked about plans for his yard, what was coming up for the community garden and a company she thought she might have convinced to partner with the garden, providing supplies it would need in exchange for being added to the posted list of their sponsors. When they pulled off I-435 onto Mer Len, Adelyn was so engrossed in the conversation, they had already pulled into the parking lot at iFly before she realized where they were headed.

She turned and stared up at the tall building in front of her. "We're going here?"

"You said no jumping out of airplanes, but you'll never be very far off the ground here, so I figured we could experience parachuting without the danger factor."

She had never thought about indoor skydiving before, but the thought intrigued her. It would be far safer, but still exciting. "It sounds like fun. Did you decide to wait on the main meal because of the schedule, or to avoid the puke factor?"

"Puke factor. I could have gotten us into a later slot, but figured we would both enjoy it more if we weren't coming in with a full stomach."

"You are a wise man." She unhooked her seatbelt and pulled her phone out of her purse while he came around to her door. She loved that he always did that, even though they weren't on a date. She got out, then tucked her purse under the seat so it would be out of sight.

"A small purse today?"

"I didn't want something bulky, in case I needed to stow or carry it." Switching everything over had almost caused her to be late for work that morning as she moved over the essentials.

"I love that you are always so prepared and plan ahead."

"It's what I do."

They walked into the building and stopped at a long counter to check in before hoofing it up several flights of stairs to the landing pad where they watched several other people take flight in the glass-surrounded wind tunnel while they waited for their training class to begin.

Adelyn studied the way the people changed position to adjust their flight height and direction, and how they shifted to land on their feet at the end of the flight—some more gracefully than others.

After a few flights, she and Jason were called into a classroom with eight other people ranging from six years old to a woman who had to be at least seventy.

Their instructor, Brian, was entertaining and dynamic without being over the top as he walked them through safety procedures. He explained more about the hand signals that would be used to guide them during their flights, and what to expect inside.

Adelyn listened closely to the directions, not wanting to mess this up. She hated making mistakes, even if it was something new.

When Brian turned to the monitor for an instructional video, Jason nudged her with his elbow. "Relax, there won't be a test afterward."

"Yes, there will, it just won't require a number two pencil," she whispered back.

The video started and she focused on the presentation again.

After receiving their flight suits and zipping them up, the group headed back to the wind tunnel and took a seat to watch the previous group finish up.

Jason volunteered to go first, having been skydiving a few times already with some Army buddies. He had opted for the high-tunnel bonus on both of his flights, where the wind was stronger, pushing you higher in the tunnel. She could hear him hooting with joy while flipping twenty feet in the air. When he finished his ride, the other people in their group were all anxious to have their turn as well—he had made it look easy. Adelyn was happy to watch a few more people go, and learn from their actions for a while longer before taking her turn.

She wasn't sure why she was so nervous—it wasn't like she was doing the high-tunnel this time, and if she decided she didn't want to on her second turn she could always tell the instructor she didn't want it. She had to admit, though, that everyone who had taken the high-tunnel option made it look like a blast and said it was the best part.

When it was her turn, Adelyn entered the tunnel and let Brian help her onto the blast of air. She kept her mouth closed to avoid the drool someone else had warned of when they came out of the tunnel, and tested out different angles of her hand and chin to regulate her height and direction. The last few seconds of the first one-minute flight, she maneuvered around to face Jason. Their eyes met and she grinned.

When she came out to join him, she still felt the adrenaline pumping through her, exhilarated by the experience. "That. Was. Amazing."

Jason slid his arm around her shoulder in a hug. "I knew you would love it. Ready to do the high tunnel next time?"

"Oh yeah. I can't wait."

It was totally worth it, she decided as she circled around in the top of the tunnel fifteen minutes later. She would have to do this again sometime. It was so much better than a roller coaster.

This time when she exited the tunnel, Jason waited to grab her into a bear hug—he was so great at those. "Thank you so much for bringing me. This was amazing!"

"You're welcome. I'm glad I could be the one to introduce you to something new, expand your horizons." He slung an arm around her shoulder and gave her a sideways hug as they returned to their seats.

"I like the expansion."

Before they changed out of their flight suits, they had one of the other flyers take a picture of the two of them and Adelyn posted it to her Facebook page. "Went indoor skydiving for the first time with Jason McCormick. Most fun I've had in years." She tagged his mom and Maddie, both of whom commented before she and Jason had finished their meal down the road at Jack Stack's Barbecue.

As Jason dropped her at her car in the otherwise empty city office parking lot that night, she gave him another big hug when he walked her to her car door, despite it being only a few feet away. "Thanks again. That was a blast."

He grinned at her, his face half exposed in the parking lot lights, half in the dark. "Any time. Seriously, I would totally make up an excuse to go again if I had to. There's nothing like a good skydive, but this comes pretty close."

Adelyn laughed. "You're awesome." She kissed him on the cheek, then turned and slid into her car.

She still felt the smoothness of his cheek on her lips when she saw him getting into his truck. She didn't know how she deserved such a great friend.

If she had felt a frisson of electricity between them a couple times that night, she could ignore it. He'd made it perfectly clear that he didn't want to date her, so they would stay just friends.

Besides, she was seeing Daniel and didn't need the confusion of being interested in more than one guy at a time.

Chapter Thirteen

"We're back!" Piper sing-songed as they walked through the doors of the wedding dress shop where they had purchased her dress that spring.

Adelyn followed on her heels with Maddie behind her and Comfrey brought up the rear. They had all met at the city offices and ridden over together in Comfrey's car.

"Your fitting isn't scheduled for a while, is it?" Jessica, the clerk who had sold Piper her dress, asked.

"No, but this time it's Maddie's turn." Piper gestured to her with a flourish. "She's getting married the week before me, so we decided we better get in here ASAP. Her mom is supposed to meet us here." Piper glanced around the group toward the front window, but the way her brow furrowed, Mrs. McCormick must not have been in sight.

"Great, come on back. I'll have a dressing room ready for you in a few minutes. Grab a drink." She gestured them to the seating area next to the one they had taken before and the clerk disappeared down the hall to the dressing room.

"Didn't you make an appointment?" Adelyn asked.

"Yes, but we're a little early," Maddie checked her watch. "I guess we were all a little anxious to get together. I've missed our weekly lunches lately, it seems like we can never mesh our schedules for girl time." She wandered over to the racks of dresses and started looking at them. "So how did things go with Jason last night? Your pictures from the skydiving simulator looked fun. How was it?"

"Really great. We had fun, and I always love Jack Stacks."

"You had a date with Jason? It's about time. Do tell." Comfrey joined them. She looked through the five dresses Maddie had pulled out and place on a rack to try on. She removed two of them and slid them to the end. "Not even. The other three are okay, though."

"Whose dress is this?" Maddie put one fist on her hip.

Comfrey gave Maddie one of those looks that said not to question her. "I know fashion and lines, even if it doesn't look like it half the time." She gestured to the rust-colored t-shirt she wore and the brown jeans. "This is not what I wore in my previous life, you know. Even if I don't get fancy very often, I still know what looks good, and those dresses, while beautiful, were not going to work."

"Your style and my style don't have to be the same."

"Oh, no. I wouldn't wear the three I left for you—they are *your* style, not mine. These might not be what you had in mind, but you should at least try them on and see what you think." She grabbed the dress Maddie had pulled out of the racks and slid it back. "This would be gorgeous on Adelyn, but it's not for you, either. Come, let me be your guide."

Maddie let out of huff of annoyance, but begrudgingly followed along.

"Now that's settled," Piper joined them, flipping through the dresses Maddie had set aside. "Tell us about the date with Jason."

"It wasn't a date, it was only a thank-you dinner. Jason took me out for helping in his yard. I thought it should be the other way around considering all the extra work we made for him with that design, but who am I to complain if he wants to pay for my meal?"

"And fake skydiving." Maddie slid another dress onto her

rolling rack after Comfrey approved it. She seemed to have accepted that it was easier this way, though the rebellious angle of her chin said she wasn't convinced that Comfrey would pick the right dress. Adelyn, however, approved of the new options on the rack. Comfrey definitely had an eye for lines and she was dead right about all the dresses so far.

"Dinner plus activity equals date." Piper shot Adelyn a speculative look. "How long have you been dating Jason?"

"I'm not dating him, we're just friends." Except there had been more than one moment when it had felt date-like. "If that's your criteria, we've been dating practically since he got home from Afghanistan."

"Mmm-hmm." Maddie was looking at another dress, which Comfrey took and put away.

"I never realized you were such a fashionista." Maddie shot Comfrey a look of annoyance.

"Normally I'd say happy colors, tints, bold patterns, but the options, wedding-dress wise are not as obvious. Still, there are lots of good ones that will work for you." Comfrey returned her gaze to the dresses on the main rack again. "Besides, I don't think that hum of agreement was about the dress."

It took Adelyn a moment to figure out what she meant. "I have not been dating Jason for months. We're *friends*. Seriously, you've all seen us together."

"Yes, yes, we have." Comfrey's words may have been pointed, but she didn't take her eyes from the dresses in front of her.

The bell over the front door rang and Eve McCormick came through, interrupting the conversation. Adelyn was torn between wanting to know what she meant by that pointed remark, and really, really not wanting to get into it with Jason's mom in the room.

"All my girls in one place." Eve greeted them each with a hug.

"Piper, Maddie showed me the picture of you in your dress—it's so perfect. I can't wait to see my baby girl all dressed up, even though I know I'm going to cry rivers." She hugged Maddie as she said this, her eyes already tearing up.

Adelyn had never seen Eve without a smile on her face—unless you counted the two times she had been very unamused at the girl's shenanigans in high school. Those were the days.

She was so glad to have them in her past.

Eve gave her a hug and complimented her hair and then hugged Comfrey. "It's been too long. Your mom called to see what you were up to a few days ago and to make sure you were okay."

"My mom? Are you sure it wasn't a prank?" Comfrey asked.

"Oh, no. It was her. I wrote her a letter after you helped get the greenhouse ready for Maddie's class last spring to tell her what a terrific daughter she had raised and how impressed we were with you. She called me the next week and we talk periodically now." Eve moved on to the dresses, agreeing with Comfrey's opinion on the two she had set apart from the rest.

Comfrey's mouth hung open in shock.

Adelyn grinned. "That's Eve—she wants every parent to know how fantastic their kids are, even when their kids are grown adults. How did she find your mom, anyway?"

"I have no idea. I didn't think I'd mentioned them."

"She's pretty good at ferreting things out. I got the impression your parents were more...standoffish to the peons like us."

"They usually are. Then again, Mom has been trying to bridge the gap a little lately. Maybe Eve is responsible. I only hear half as many complaints about my single status and lifestyle choices these days."

"The joys of being the only single daughter. My mom will never be happy with my choices, either." Adelyn shot Comfrey a commiserating look.

"As long as we're happy, right?" Comfrey said, but she shot Eve another glance, clearly not sure how to deal with the new information.

"You know it."

The clerk bustled back to them, her arms full of dresses. "Sorry, there was a bit of a mess back there. I've got it cleared out now. Have you found some dresses you like?"

"I've found a lot, but these are the ones the others approved as well." Maddie said, shooting them a dirty look.

"Great choices. Let me add a couple more." The clerk searched through several racks, plucking out dresses as she went, and added four to the rolling rack.

She and Maddie went back to the dressing room while the others settled into the chairs to enjoy a bottled water and snack.

"So how are things going with the wedding setup?" Eve asked Adelyn. "Jason said you finished the major landscaping install, but he thinks like a man, so I know there's more to do."

Adelyn laughed. "Yes. There's more, but the major stuff is in place. I was looking at decorations that we can change out for each of the brides, and we're planting four huge planters on rollers on the west side of the house—two for each wedding theme. I should swing by there after we finish tonight to make sure he's watering them properly. It's been getting hot lately."

"You're a wonder. I'm so impressed with everything you do. Before you know it, it'll be you trying on dresses."

Adelyn felt embarrassed at the praise, though it meant more to her than if it had come from almost anyone else. "Thanks, but I've only been on two dates with Daniel, I think it's a little premature to be planning a wedding."

"Who's Daniel?" Eve tipped her head to the side.

"The guy I just started dating."

"Hmm."

Confused that Eve had expected her to get married soon when she didn't seem to know Adelyn was dating anyone, she continued the yard discussion with some of the minutia on the decorations. She used her tablet to show everyone pictures she had pinned online and was happy with their feedback.

The discussion lasted through the first four dresses, and then Maddie came out in the perfect Ivory creation. The tulle skirt was full with a short train and large, white embroidered flowers adding some fun to the style. The flowers were echoed, much smaller, on the bodice, which had a reasonably demure V-neck and wide shoulder straps that showed off her peaches and cream complexion. It was perfect for her in every way.

Eve clutched her pearls and tears rose to her eyes as Maddie turned around a couple times to catch every detail in the mirrors and show the others.

"It's perfect," Comfrey said. "Don't you think?"

"So perfect–and it's twenty-percent off because it's on closeout!"

"How can you get better than that?" Adelyn asked. "This beats the others hands down, and they would have been very nice."

They fiddled with veils and tiaras, finally finding one of each that would be perfect for Maddie and the dress.

"Okay, I must have some sugar after taxing my credit card like that," Eve said. "How about if I buy?"

"Because your credit card needs a little more of a workout?" Comfrey asked.

"Because it needs to cool off slowly, like stretching after you exercise, and a trip to Sweet Confections is what the doctor ordered."

Adelyn couldn't agree more.

The bakery would close in less than an hour, but it was still packed with Saturday night dates. The five of them managed to find a table they could all squeeze around, even if it was a little tight.

Rachel was at the counter, but busy with an incoming call when they came in. She came over a few minutes later to see how they were doing. "It looks like you're all settled in with some deliciousness. Is this a celebration?"

"That we survived," Comfrey agreed. "We all went wedding dress shopping with Maddie."

"Really?" Rachel checked out Maddie's ring. "I heard rumors, but I haven't seen you for a while. Congratulations. Marriage is pretty awesome. If you find the right guy, it's totally worth the hassle of the wedding."

"I'm glad to hear that. Even with Adelyn on double-wedding patrol, it's been a little hectic finalizing details."

"It always is." Rachel turned to Adelyn. "Grayson said you were at Noodles and Brisket lately with a new guy. Anyone special?" She wiggled her brows.

"Maybe, I haven't decided yet."

"With so many options to choose from, you're bound to choose right."

The phone started ringing again behind the counter and Rachel excused herself to answer it.

"So many options?" Adelyn hadn't dated anyone else for a long time, unless you count the fish guy, which she didn't.

"I think she meant Jason," Comfrey said as she scooped up another bite of cake. "You two have been out and about together a lot lately."

"Because of the wedding plans for those two." Adelyn gestured to Piper and Maddie.

"Of course." But there was a tinge of doubt in her voice.

Dating Jason? Everyone must be losing their minds.

What was with her tonight? Adelyn decided to turn the tables. "How was your date with Tony?"

"Date with Tony? What date with Tony? Why haven't I heard about it?" Piper asked.

"It wasn't a big deal." Comfrey shrugged, though she seemed less awkward about it than Adelyn had felt.

"But you two had a date?" Eve asked.

"It was the bachelor auction. He was about to be purchased by Tiffany Trainer. After what she tried to help Layla do to Piper, do you really think Tony deserved that fate? So I bid on him. We went out. It was fun. We managed a lunch date last week. We plan to do it again—as soon as we can mesh our schedules. The community garden, getting my property ready for goats, and working with the wo-men's shelter has kept me busy. He's been traveling for work more than usual too."

"If it was really something, you would have found an excuse to go out with him again," Adelyn insisted.

"I don't know. The man can *kiss*. It's definitely worth testing the dating waters some more."

"Whoa, you go girl. So there *is* more to tell than you're letting on," Maddie said.

"Maybe, maybe not. Good chemistry is important, and can make the rest of the relationship easier, but it's not the most important thing. Trust me, I've learned the hard way. There's a lot more for us to explore. But I like him."

"Here's to exploring." Piper lifted her paper cup of hot cocoa and the others followed suit, tapping rims.

Chapter Fourteen

"No way, I would never really skydive, even though the tunnel was a blast." Adelyn grinned at Daniel over their ice cream. Ralphie was swinging in the backyard, and the two of them sat on the deck, scooping up the last of their treat. Ralphie had already finished his and run back out to enjoy the sunny afternoon.

"But you enjoyed it."

"So. Much. Isn't that crazy? But now I've tried that, I'm thinking my bucket list has taken on whole new proportions. For example: Is there an alternative to bungee jumping that's safe and not crazy? What about swimming with the sharks?"

"Or swimming with alligators. Because clearly, one dangerous hobby deserves another." He shook his head. "I think I'd rather stick to normal stuff. How about you, when is your next great adventure?"

Adelyn considered that as her spoon quested for the last dollop of creamy goodness. "You wouldn't happen to have a riding lawn mower, would you?"

"Um, yeah. There's nothing exciting about that. I use it all the time."

"So true, but have you ever done a tractor pull?"

"A tractor pull? Like at those redneck fairs?"

She sat up a little taller in her seat, trying not to show her annoyance. "The fair is not redneck. It's traditional. And tractor pulls are fun. I enter every year at the Founder's Day celebration. You should bring yours out and join me."

"Um, I think I'll pass." He studied her for a moment, tipping his head to the side. "I never thought of you as the tractor-pull type."

"I have many facets you have yet to explore." She was disappointed that he wouldn't step an inch outside his comfort zone to try the tractor pull, but decided not to let it derail her—she wasn't going to stick to her list on everything. Besides, maybe he would be into a lot of new experiences that didn't involve lawn tractors.

"Your friend Comfrey contacted me this morning."

"She's always prompt. What did you decide?"

"It sounds good. There are so many special programs for single moms and other women, it's a shame more of them don't try to branch out on their own."

"When are you speaking?"

"The seventeenth. Would you come along to support me?" He twined their fingers together.

"Sure, from the back row. I'll totally cheer you on."

"Who knows, maybe I'll inspire you to branch out and start your own business. As involved as you are in your friends' weddings, you might want to try a career as a wedding planner." He squeezed her hand.

"No, thank you, I'm perfectly fine where I am. Knowing more about programs that are available might help me with some of the people who come through my office to get information about starting a business, though. I appreciate you being willing to help—it's an extraordinary group of women, considering the struggles they've been through. I admire them so much. My life has been a picnic in comparison."

"I'm sure you've had a few things to overcome yourself."

Adelyn shrugged. Sure, she hadn't exactly lived a cake walk, but there were struggles and then there was what Sheila and some of the others had been through. There was no comparison.

She glanced at her watch. It was coming up on five. They had eaten a late lunch and she wasn't at all hungry, but her mom was expecting her for Sunday dinner soon. "I probably better get going or my mom will start calling to find out why I'm not thirty minutes early."

"You always go early?"

"I tend to run a little ahead of schedule. Plus my Uncle Mark is supposed to be there, and I can't wait to see him. He's been living out of state for a long time."

"I wouldn't want to get in the way."

"Oh please, you're not in the way. I had a good time this afternoon. Thanks for inviting me."

"It was almost as good as a Saturday night date."

She grinned since he had tried to get together with her the previous night, but she had already been scheduled. "It's hard to get between me and my besties. We found the perfect dress for Maddie, though. Fun and lovely at the same time."

"As long as I was turned down for a good reason." He smiled and winked as she stood. He stood as well, and called to Ralphie that he would be back soon. They left him in the fenced yard, heading through the house to the front door. It was a charming place, a twenty-something rambler with popcorn ceilings and ivory kitchen appliances. It felt comfortable and lived in, but not cluttered. It could use an update or two, but that wasn't really important.

"So, how does Thursday look?" he asked.

"That's the tractor pull, but you can join me. Also, the

community garden will be doing a big picking tomorrow, if you want to bring Ralphie and help out. We can always use a few extra hands, and maybe we could grab a snack after."

"That sounds good. What time?"

"Six-thirty."

"Perfect." Daniel set his hands on her hips and drew her closer. "I'm having such a good time with you."

"I am too. Thanks for inviting me over." Adelyn slid easily into his arms, smoothing her hands over his chest. It was nice, not muscular, but not flabby either, and he smelled good. It had been a long time since her last kiss—not that she hadn't had opportunities here and there, but she hadn't been interested enough to let them try recently. She let herself melt into his embrace. Daniel was a few inches taller than she was, even in her three-inch wedges, so their mouths met nicely. He had nice form and as his hands slid up her back, she pressed a little closer.

It was a great setup—the almost-perfect guy, good technique, and some attraction, but his kiss didn't thrill her the way she had hoped.

Still, she did her best to enjoy the experience, genuinely sad to pull back. Kissing was fun—she'd forgotten how fun, and she did like him a lot.

"I'll see you tomorrow night," he said, drawing back with some reluctance.

"Yes, bring some gardening gloves if you have them and we'll send you home with a few veggies."

"Sounds great."

She grinned and turned down the sidewalk to her car. Maybe kissing was like her list—her expectations were too high. It was a very nice kiss. She would accept that as enough for now.

Jason arrived at the community garden several minutes before anyone else. He took his usual tour of the plots, checking to make sure the drip system was still working and that nobody's plants were withering in the hot summer sun. The humidity made him feel like withering, but the plants didn't seem overly affected by it, which was a relief. He turned the sprinkler on plot thirteen and noticed a leak in the tube, which meant half the plot was wet and the other half stayed dry, so he pulled out some tape and wrapped it. Then he made a note to do a permanent fix for the hose at the end of the season. So far it was the first problem they had run across, and he couldn't complain about that.

Maddie walked into the garden, shortly followed by a gaggle of little girls, and a trio of boys. Five minutes later Adelyn arrived, holding hands with a man Jason had never seen before. Was this Daniel, and was this a third date, or a fourth? A young boy Jason guessed to be three or four years old followed behind them, his eyes glued to a gaming device.

The man with Adelyn turned and said something to the boy and he passed the device to his father before following Adelyn into the garden. She partnered him up with an older child before making the rounds to talk to a few people.

As always, she looked totally put together—her jewelry coordinated with the medium blue top and dark blue jeans. He tried not to pay attention as she moved around the garden, instead, focusing on the tomatoes he was picking, but it didn't work very well. He was drawn to her.

Half an hour passed before she made her way over to him, carrying an empty basket.

"It's looking good," she said. "I'm impressed with how well the harvest is going so early in the summer."

I'm glad you're pleased. Who's your friend?" He indicated the guy with a tip of his head, though he was pretty sure he already knew.

"Daniel Bond. He said he was interested in what we're doing here."

"It's nice of him to join us." It took nearly everything he had to not strangle himself on the sentence.

"He's a great guy." She tucked her hands in her back pockets as they stood awkwardly across from each other.

"My yard could use some more weeding. You up for it on Thursday?"

"Sorry, can't. I have serious plans."

"What, are you going out with *Daniel?*"

"No, I have other plans, at the fair."

"That's where I was thinking of taking you."

Her brows lowered and returned quickly, and her lashes fluttered in surprise. "Well, you can come watch me in the tractor pull. Or you can join me."

"Join you on your tractor, or on my tractor?"

"I was thinking of us both being contestants. On our own tractors."

"Is *Daniel* participating?" He couldn't keep the tone of derision completely out of his voice. *Maybe* he hadn't tried as hard as he could have.

"No, he's too cool for tractor pulls. How about you?"

"Is this a bucket list kind of thing?"

She shrugged and shook her head. "I've done it before, much to my mother's dismay. I actually like it."

Jason glanced up and saw the disapproval on Daniel's face as he watched Jason and Adelyn talking. Jason turned his full-wattage smile on her. "I'd love to participate. I'll get my lawn mower tuned up."

"Perfect." Her grin was genuine as she swapped baskets with him and headed to the front to unload the veggies he had already picked.

Jason glanced at Daniel again, who met his gaze questioningly. They held the stare for a moment before Daniel looked away. Jason felt ridiculously superior that he had won the staring match.

If Adelyn was still dating Daniel, Jason needed to step up his game. The Crystal Creek Founder's Day Fair sounded like just the thing he needed.

Tuesday Adelyn looked up from her phone call to find Jason standing in the doorway to her office. She smiled and waved him in, gesturing him to take one of the cushy seats across from her. She finished taking the complaint from a woman who had bought a home near the train tracks and was always calling about the noise, and turned to him, glad to see someone friendly.

"This is a surprise," she said after she was finally allowed to hang up.

"I thought I should get all my paperwork filed for the new business before I sign contracts with Darla to start her house."

"Good call." She reached out to take the proffered paperwork. He could have filed it online, but that could take an extra day while she waited for confirmation on the fee. "It's nice to see a happy face."

"Rough day?"

"Mandy is sick so I'm dealing with her phone calls as well as my own." She read through the paperwork, making sure that everything was filled out properly. Smiling, she set it on the desk. "Everything is in order." She filled out her end of the paperwork and gave him a copy of the document.

"It'll still take a few days for the official certificate to get to you, but this is good enough to get started. You should celebrate—this is a great step."

"I think you're right. Want to grab some lunch with me?" He kept it casual, but expectant—their dinner at Jack Stacks still lived in his memory, and he hoped they would have another moment like that, however brief. Maybe it would even make her think twice about whether or not she should be dating Daniel.

He could always dream, right?

"I get my lunch break in five minutes—as soon as Audrey gets back. You have excellent timing."

"I'm pretty lucky." If lucky was a synonym for strategic planning. "Do you want me to wait out there while you grab your things?"

"No need for that. You can wait here. I just need to get this entered into the system."

Five minutes stretched into ten, but when they walked out the door, everything for his business license was properly filed, so he could hardly complain. Besides, he was getting lunch with his favorite person on the planet.

Chapter Fifteen

Dark smoke from lawn mower exhaust wafted through the air from an old machine accompanying the low growl of engines. Adelyn putted into the competition ring on Clark's shiny green John Deere and headed for the sign-in desk.

She saw Jason already there, filling out his form at the check-in desk. He looked up before she arrived and gave her a quick wave. Adelyn pulled her mower to the side and cut the power. Thankfully, her mom's house was less than a mile away so she hadn't ridden very far.

She scanned the crowd as she approached the table, searching for Daniel, but didn't see him. He said he would come, but it was still quite early, so she focused back on her destination, and the tall, dark, and handsome man who was waiting for her there. She felt a flutter in her chest and ruthlessly fought it down.

"You made it," she greeted.

"I told you I would. I always keep my word."

"I know. I almost didn't get here, though. Mom wasn't in love with the idea of me using her lawn mower—they bought it only a couple months ago and Clark has barely used it. She was afraid I'd hurt it or something."

His lips twitched. "A seasoned competitor like you? Never."

"That's what I said. As you can see, I did prevail."

"I'm not surprised. You could talk your way around nearly anyone."

She bumped him with her shoulder, and reached for a blank entry form. She recognized the woman sitting behind the table as one of the checkers at the grocery store. Natalie was also one of the women Adelyn had talked to about starting a small business a couple weeks earlier. "He's sweet, isn't he? It's good to see you here—how did you get roped into this?"

"My boss is on the festival committee and badgered me until I agreed."

"What?" A slightly balding man said as he joined them. Adelyn recognized the grocery store owner. "I may have asked nicely a couple times."

"Per day. For a week. But it sounded interesting, I guess. And since Comfrey canceled the gardening class tonight, I figured I might as well come."

"She canceled? Why?"

"She said she had some personal stuff come up and sent us all text messages yesterday when I was at work. He jumped on it." She nodded toward her boss with a tip of her head.

"You can't let helping hands go to waste, you know." He seemed unrepentant.

"I agree. I'm a big fan of nagging for volunteers."

"That's true," Jason added. "She's an excellent nagger. The queen of naggers."

"When did I ever have to nag you to do anything?" Adelyn glanced up from her entry form.

"Um..." It took him a long moment to think of something. "Four years ago, when you wanted me to make a corner shelf for your bathroom."

"That was more wheedling than nagging."

"Po-tay-to po-tah-to." Jason passed over a twenty. "I'll handle both our entry fees."

"You don't have to do that," Adelyn tried to pay with a ten-dollar bill.

"I know. See you at the scale." He left the twenty on the table, tapped two fingers to the brim of his Royals ball cap, and headed toward the right.

Adelyn only let herself watch him for a few seconds before focusing back on her entry form, which was still mostly empty.

"Lucky you," Natalie said.

"What do you mean?" Adelyn asked.

"He's so into you. Seriously, I'd be all over that man given half a chance."

Adelyn's brows crinkled. "Jason? McCormick? Are you serious?"

"You don't think he's a catch?"

"Well, yeah. He'd be a great catch. He's a terrific guy, but I think you're misreading the situation. We're not dating, and he's not interested in me. We're just friends."

"Um, beg to differ."

"Beg all you want." Natalie was clearly crazy, Adelyn thought as she signed the bottom of her form and passed it over.

The woman held an expression that said she didn't believe a word of it, but she wasn't going to argue. Adelyn took her tag and thanked her, then headed for her tractor. She needed to weigh in.

The scale was an on-your-honor thing. A short ramp led on one side and off the next and the riders were responsible to make sure they weren't over the weight limit.

Jason was several people ahead of her and she saw him pull up onto the scale and wait for it to register. He leaned back and pulled a flat weight from a weight set off the back and toss it to the side, then looked back again. One more joined the first on the ground beside the scale and he nodded, then drove down the ramp. He pulled out of the way, then stopped to get off and retrieve the weights.

Adelyn knew some people took this event very seriously—going so far as to put a souped-up engine from a truck in their tractors to give them extra distance—but she hadn't expected Jason to go to the extra effort of adding weight to his mower on his first try.

Then again, he could be a tad competitive. She kept the chuckle to herself as she recalled the class competition in school during Homecoming week. He had downed that peanut butter and bologna sandwich like it was nothing—winning the competition hands down. Afterward he said it was the grossest thing he'd ever eaten. She inched forward in the growing lineup. It was a good thing she had arrived early.

The John Deere was well within the weight limit, which had Adelyn wishing she had brought along a few extra weights as well, but she gave it up. Surely with the new engine in her mower, she would still perform well.

The track was being groomed by a large tractor with tank-tread wheels and a blade, tamping the dirt down and scraping it reasonably smooth. They would repack the ground between each run to give the competitors all an equal chance at scoring well.

Two kids ran across the track area in shorts and cowboy boots, the girl wearing a bright red cowboy hat that matched her flowered top. They approached a couple of men standing at the end of the track, and both were scooped into strong male arms. By the time Adelyn reached Jason—who was stretched out with his sneakers dangling over the mower engine—the kids were settled on tiny tractors and headed for the weigh-in. As if there was any chance they would be over-weight. But she supposed that was part of the fun.

She drove past Jason, and with a little trouble, backed into the place beside him. "I didn't expect you to get into this enough to add weights."

"I didn't expect you to come in shorts, cowboy boots, and a tee sporting the festival theme."

"Hey, I own western boots. I just don't wear them very often."

"You are a constant surprise."

She didn't know how she could be when they had known each other for so long. "A woman has to retain a little mystery now and then."

"Speaking of mysteries. Your date's over there with his kid." Jason motioned with a tip of his head.

Adelyn looked around him to see Daniel and Ralphie approaching. She grinned and waved to them. They waved back and in a moment were stopping in front of her.

"You look like you fit in perfectly here," Daniel said.

"She fits in pretty much anywhere; being smart and beautiful will do that for a woman," Jason said amiably.

Daniel's gaze darted toward him, as if taken a little by surprise. "Yes, that's true. You do look great. I don't think I've seen you dressed nearly so casually before."

Adelyn grinned. "I do wear my work clothes most of the time. Did you just get here, or have you had a good chance to look around?"

"We've only been here a few minutes. We had to come see how things were going first."

His son tugged at Daniel's arm. "Dad, you promised me a funnel cake."

"After the tractor pull so Adelyn can join us."

"That sounds great. I love funnel cake," Adelyn agreed.

"Yeah she does. Back in high school—" Jason's words cut off as Adelyn leaned over and covered his mouth with her hand.

She glared at him, managing to keep her expression lethal despite the glint of fun in his eyes. “Don’t you even think about repeating that story. Not ever.”

His lips curved under her fingers and he used his hand to cross his heart and held it up in testimony, though he could totally have gotten away if he’d wanted to.

She shot him another warning glare and moved her hand away. Turning back to Daniel, she forced a smile. “Anyway, funnel cake is great. I’d be happy to join you.”

“Good to hear it.” Daniel said, but he shot a look at Jason, like he wasn’t sure what to think about him. “Have you known each other long?”

“Oh, yeah. He’s Maddie’s older brother, so he was always around when we were growing up, a lot like the obnoxious big brother you wish you could get away from.”

“You don’t seem to feel that way anymore.” Daniel’s eyes narrowed on them.

“No, we got past that by the time she started college,” Jason said. “We’re definitely better friends now than we used to be. We hang out quite a lot.”

Adelyn was afraid Daniel would get the wrong idea and amended, “The whole group of us hang out together. We’re both on the board for the community garden.”

“Plus she’s been helping me get my yard ready for Piper’s and Maddie’s weddings this summer. That’s been a lot of work,” Jason said.

“Lucky for us, there are a lot of extra helpers around to spread it around.” What was he doing, trying to sabotage her relationship?

“Sounds like you have a tight group of friends.” Daniel’s expression had turned warier as they spoke, though the shift had been subtle.

"We do. I feel so lucky," Adelyn admitted. "The others should be around here tonight as well. I'm sure we'll run into them."

The speakers made a low thudding sound as they came on and the announcer's voice thundered out that the event would start in five minutes.

"I guess we should go find a spot," Daniel said.

"Don't rush, they'll start with the littlest kids first, so it'll be a while before we get our turns."

"Good to know. Good luck!" Daniel gave her a little wave, then headed out of the fenced area and around to the stands.

"What was that all about?" Adelyn asked Jason as soon as she was sure Daniel couldn't hear.

"What?" Jason adjusted the bill of his cap.

"Don't play coy with me. You know exactly what I mean. Why were you making him think there was something more than friendship between us?"

There were several seconds filled with the noise of tractors and a few voices calling across the grounds before Jason finally responded. "I said that we spend time together, and that you've been helping me out. If it sounded like there's more between us than friendship, well, I can't help that."

That hadn't been the answer she was looking for and Adelyn waffled for a moment, studying him and the long look he was giving her. Normally he had a smile in his voice when he was teasing her, but there was no smile now.

"What do you mean?"

Jason put his feet down and leaned forward across the steering wheel. "Maybe friendship isn't the only thing between us, Adelyn. It's time you considered that."

"No. We're friends. We're definitely not more than friends. Guys and girls can just be friends and nothing else."

"Can they? A single guy and a single girl. Can they really be as close as we've become and stay nothing but friends? I'm not so sure about that."

"Are you saying..." Adelyn closed her mouth, not wanting to voice the words because if he answered the way she feared he was going to, then things were going to get very, very awkward between them for a while and she couldn't afford that so close to the weddings.

"Spit it out if you want an answer." Jason didn't take his gaze from her face.

Adelyn looked away and caught sight of Daniel and his son sitting on bleachers across the way. Daniel waved when she looked his way. He had obviously been watching.

Adelyn waved back as they announced the winner of the tots' competition and called the first three people to line up for the adult section.

"You're not going to ask," Jason said after a couple minutes.

"No, I think it would be better if I didn't."

"Wow, I never thought you were chicken."

Adelyn was trying to decide on a retort when Natalie from the registration table came through with a clipboard. "Adelyn, you'll be after Bobby there and Mr. McCormick will be three spots after that."

"Thanks." Adelyn started her engine again, needing an excuse to put space between them. "I think I'll go wait in line."

"It'll be a while," Natalie advised.

"That's all right. I'm kind of anxious to get going."

She didn't look at Jason again, though she heard him call good luck to her as she drove away. Jason McCormick did *not* have a crush on her. They did not have a romantic relationship, and they never would. He turned her down for a date a few months ago.

There was no way any of that meant what she thought it might. And if it did, that was too bad. She was happy with the new guy she was seeing. The end. That was it. No more.

But when she looked back at Jason, she couldn't help wondering for a fleeting second if kissing him would be any more exciting than kissing Daniel.

He was already talking to the man on his other side. She had no idea what she would say when she spoke to him next. Hopefully it wouldn't be tonight because she had no idea what to think at the moment.

Jason watched Adelyn as she hooked her mower up to the sled for her turn. He felt a little like she had tried to cut out his heart with a knife. How could she have been so clueless about how he felt for her—and how could she have refused to even ask if he was interested in her—he'd waited, anxiety shooting through him as she had debated whether or not she cared enough to hear the truth.

Or had she been too scared to ask? But why would she be scared—it wasn't her heart on the line.

Adelyn waved to everyone in the stands—which now included Maddie and Ben as well as Daniel—did they ever go out without the kid around? Not that he had a problem with kids—he liked kids, but it was a lot harder to have a serious conversation with a preschooler breaking in constantly. He was still amazed that Ben and Maddie managed to have real conversations as often as Felicia interrupted them. Then again, Ben and Maddie made sure to have time together when Felicia was with family or at a friend's house.

Adelyn's tractor pulled forward, moving easily at first, and then slowing as the load rose on the sled behind her. The further she pulled, the higher the weight lifted, which increased the pressure on the mower. The sled also measured the distance she had traveled, so the judges were able to get accurate readings for each contestant.

The mower really started to slow down at one hundred feet, and Adelyn leaned forward, her lips moving as if she could convince it to add a few extra feet to the distance. The light of competition brightened her face and for the first time Jason didn't have to wonder why she had been drawn to the event.

She passed the previous contestants' distances, reaching a full eight feet beyond the furthest, then did a little celebration in her seat when she couldn't pull any further and her distance was announced. He grinned despite himself.

She was something else.

Jason didn't think he could let things go back to normal between them, even if she could pretend their conversation hadn't happened. He decided to give her the night—soon he was going to make his feelings crystal clear. She had been on a date tonight, so his timing had been off.

At least if she rejected him after that, he would know that it was him, and not her obliviousness or his anxiety that kept them apart.

Chapter Sixteen

Adelyn waited until Jason beat her distance record before shutting down the mower where it would be out of the way for the evening. She went looking for Daniel and Ralphie. She didn't want to think about the conversation with Jason right now. At this moment, she wanted to focus on Daniel and see where it might go. It would have been easier if she could have pursued the relationship without Jason's words reverberating through her head, but she would do her best.

"So, how did you like your first tractor pull?" she asked when she met Daniel and Ralphie a few minutes later.

"It's boring." Ralphie tugged on his dad's hand. "Can we get funnel cake now?"

Daniel was more tactful. "I think it's the kind of event that is probably more exciting for the participants."

Adelyn chuckled. "That it is, which is why I'm going with you instead of waiting for everyone else to take their turns. How do you like your funnel cake?"

"With fruit and powdered sugar. It's yummy that way," Ralphie said.

"So true. I can't believe anyone likes it any other way," she agreed.

She walked along with father and son making comments about

the booths, greeting people as they walked past, and keeping an eye out for her friends. Maddie and Ben hadn't been watching the tractor pull when Adelyn joined Daniel, though they had been when Jason took his turn.

"I've got a babysitter lined up for the evening I present to the women's group," Daniel said when Ralphie was focused on a ring toss game a while later. "Would you like to join me for dessert afterward?"

A second date for the two of them without his son? That sounded great. She liked Ralphie, alone time would also be welcome. "That sounds great. I'm definitely in."

"Good."

Adelyn waved to someone from work and caught sight of Jason talking to Maddie—the conversation looked serious, and when Jason looked up at her, he didn't seem happy to see her and looked away again almost immediately.

Adelyn clamped her jaw shut and turned back to her date. Whatever Jason's problem, it wasn't her issue.

"Is something going on with you and Jason?" Daniel asked a moment later when they stood in line for the much-anticipated funnel cakes. "You two looked kind of serious after I left, and he implied that maybe I'm stepping on his toes."

"That was kind of weird, I'm not sure why he implied that." She didn't want to get into it—especially since she didn't understand it herself.

"But you two don't have something going on that I should know about? You didn't used to date or anything?"

"No, we've never dated. I promise." She smiled and set a reassuring hand on his arm. When he smiled and looked relieved, she wished she could calm her own concerns so easily.

On the way to an empty picnic table with their bounty, Adelyn caught sight of Comfrey. With a guy Adelyn had never seen before or heard about. Her curiosity was piqued, so when Comfrey came into sight again a moment later with the man, Adelyn waved and they met in the middle.

"Hi, Comfrey, I know you talked with Daniel on the phone, but I thought you might like to meet in person, since you're here anyway."

Comfrey smiled and greeted Daniel with a handshake before turning to introduce Mr. tall, dark, and handsome. "Nick, this is Adelyn Shaw and Daniel Bond. Adelyn, this is Nick, an old friend from home. He's in the area for work for a few days and dropped in to say hi."

"It's great to meet you. She didn't say she had an *old friend* coming to visit," Adelyn said. Nick—wasn't that her ex-boyfriend's name?

"I kind of sprung it on her at the last minute. Chance and I are getting married."

Adelyn was confused at first, then based on the way he was looking at Comfrey, realized who he was talking about.

Before Adelyn could react to the announcement, Comfrey corrected him. "We're not engaged anymore. We broke up. Four years ago."

"You never officially broke it off when you ran away."

Comfrey looked more than a little aggravated.

Adelyn studied them both. "Her name isn't Chance."

"Comfrey is a name she chose for herself, it's not her real name," he pointed out.

"I know, I processed her business license." Comfrey's real name was Channing, which Adelyn thought was pretty. She could see how the nickname connected, but wondered how it had come about.

"It's a long story." Nick slid an arm around Comfrey's waist and she looked like she wasn't sure how she felt about it being there—but she didn't pull away.

"I love long stories. I'll have to catch up with you on that one. How long are you going to be in town?"

"A while, I'll be working remotely for the time being. This is a pretty area. I can see why she likes it so much."

"Thanks, it's a great place to live." Adelyn could see Comfrey was anxious to get away, for whatever reason. "I'll catch up with you in the next few days."

"Yeah, that would be great. Thanks."

The couple said goodbye to Adelyn, Daniel, and his son before melting back into the crowd.

"She looks a little anxious," Daniel said.

"Yeah, weird. I knew she had gotten serious with someone years back, but I thought it was way over. Apparently there's a lot more story for me to coax out of her."

"You always coax stories out of people?"

"If they're my good friends, I do. Especially when it's clear they need to talk, even if they don't want to."

"Dad, aren't you done yet?" Ralphie had scarfed down his funnel cake in record time, while the adults were only a quarter into theirs.

"Patience. We'll get out to see the rest of the fair." Daniel looked at his son with amused exasperation.

Adelyn glanced back at where Comfrey was talking to a soap vendor. She was holding Nick's hand, so obviously she still liked him, but Adelyn definitely needed more details.

Chapter Seventeen

Adelyn bent over the plant, grabbing the vines and wrapping them around the trellises that she and Jason had set up. His truck pulled into the driveway as she finished the first one and moved to the next corner of the pergola.

She hesitated for a moment before turning to wave to him. For the past several days she had been thinking about that moment during the tractor pull when he had indicated he was interested in her as more than a friend, and she had refused to ask him straight out, like the wimp she was. Though she had considered confronting him about it, she had finally decided it was best if she let it go.

She wasn't going to give up on Daniel, and very likely ruin her friendship with Jason—and she had seen all of her parents' many breakups with their spouses and other significant partners. None of them liked each other anymore and she couldn't stand to ruin what she had with Jason.

Jason waved back, but took a moment before he exited the truck and walked over. "I didn't expect to see you."

"I wanted to check on the plants. I noticed last time I was here that some of the vines were nearly ready for training. I know you've got a lot of other things on your mind with the new business, and I figured I could use half an hour in the evening air working in your garden to unwind."

"Rough day?"

"No more than usual, I guess. I felt itchy and needed to get out for a while without a lot of people around or my phone ringing."

"You don't have your phone?" He shot her a look of mock horror.

"Very funny. It's in the car, but no one needs to get a hold of me so badly that it can't wait half an hour." She focused back on the vines, twining them around and using a piece of flexible wrap to keep it in place while it sent out tendrils to adhere itself to the wood. She was grateful that he had allowed her to pretend like the previous conversation hadn't happened.

"The weeds are starting to be a problem too."

"Thus why I've been here thirty minutes already and I'm nowhere near halfway done. You want to join me?" Though a part of her wanted him to leave her alone so she wouldn't have to feel uncomfortable, if she was going to pretend that their previous discussion never happened, then she needed to slide back into the normal routine tonight.

Besides, she could have misunderstood him. Couldn't she?

Adelyn glanced over and smiled when Jason set his stuff down and started work on the other corner.

"How are things coming for Darla's house?"

"We're about ready to file a building permit. I need another hour or so to finalize the paperwork. I think. It's kind of a pain."

"Yeah, nothing can be easy, right? She's so excited about the house. Do you have your subs lined up?"

"Yeah I'll start digging the foundation as soon as the permit is approved. The cement guys will be hard on my heels. They already have the go-ahead on the loan so we're about ready to start."

"It's all coming together. I was starting to wonder if you were going to finally become a contractor or work for Peter forever."

"Hey, I have goals and dreams. And you missed it, since you wandered off, but did you hear that I came in third place on the tractor pull?"

"That's great. I didn't hear the final standings. I knew that several of the other guys would totally kick my tail though, and Ralphie was getting antsy to get out and see everything. You know how it is when you're a kid."

"Yeah. There's not enough time to see everything out there. I still feel that way sometimes."

"It's the best way to be."

"Is there anything else we need to do for the yard besides basic maintenance between now and the weddings?" Jason asked.

"I'm keeping an eye on those flowers around the pond. If they don't start to fill in soon, we'll have to crowd a few more in to fill it properly, but otherwise, it's just weeding and training vines."

"What about other parts of the wedding?"

"Oddly enough, the brides mostly wanted me to focus here while they planned most of their weddings themselves." She shot him a grin. "I decided not to be offended that they don't want me running the show, but I'm sure we'll come up with some more to help with as it grows closer. I can't believe it's already July."

"And muggy with it. I was surprised to see you in your skirt out here, looking all pressed and elegant in your bare feet."

"What can I say, skirts are comfy, and I didn't want to go home first."

"Have you eaten yet?"

Adelyn looked at him and hesitated for a heartbeat or two before admitting she hadn't.

"I have some cardboard pizza in the freezer if you want to join me."

"With a description like that, how can I turn you down?" She knew the cardboard referred to the packaging, not the crust—at least that was usually the case, but she still had to tease him.

"If you prefer, I do have bread and peanut butter."

"I think I can handle pizza." They shared a smile and he went inside to start the oven.

She had been so afraid that things would be awkward and bad between them, it was a relief to find out that they could return to their old rhythm.

Now if she could only put the thought out of her head that he saw her as more than a buddy.

He should have been happy that things were back on an even keel with Adelyn—thrilled even. He had been afraid that he'd totally mucked things up with her at the tractor pull, and a little time and distance made him question what he had been thinking. How could he have risked their friendship like that when it was clear that she wasn't interested in him?

So why, after a great, casual evening with her, had he been unable to sleep properly? He'd drifted off, then awoken several times before two. Then he had woken from a flashback nightmare and lay in the dark for twenty ridiculously slow minutes.

Finally he got up. There was no point in lying there in the dark when he knew he wasn't going to sleep again anytime soon.

He had a few pieces of exercise equipment at home for when he just needed a quick workout, but he was too keyed up, and needed a trip to the gym—not an uncommon occurrence since returning from his latest deployment to Afghanistan. Thankfully there was an all-night gym only a few miles away and at night the traffic was nearly non-existent.

Jason used his key code to get through the door and noticed a few other people were there, despite the insane hour. He waved to a woman across the room who worked closing shift at a local gas station and then settled in to the lat bar, greeting Tyler Jackson, who was doing squats nearby. “We have to quit meeting like this.”

Tyler grinned. “I haven’t been off work that long. What’s your excuse?” They had known each other since high school and had even been in Afghanistan at the same base for several months when their deployments had overlapped.

“Sometimes my brain still thinks it has to be on maneuvers at this hour.”

“Tell me about it.” Tyler grimaced. “Charlee said you’re putting out your own shingle. She’s sorry to lose you as a sub.”

“It’s been great working with and for her, but I was ready to move out on my own, I’m a little slower than she is.”

Tyler’s sister, Charlee, had branched out from the construction company they had both been working for only a few months ago. Thankfully the economy in the area seemed to be headed in an upward trend, so there was work to go around.

“I understand.”

The rest of the hour before Tyler left, they occasionally swapped sports comments or talked about other things that came to mind, but most of the time they worked out silently, in the same area, but not exactly together. That was fine for Jason. As soon as he settled into his rhythm on the machines, his mind drifted to Adelyn.

Could he be happy if she married someone else without him laying it on the line for her?

Considering his nightmares, sleeplessness, and occasional episodes of PTSD, would it be fair to pursue anything anyway? He couldn’t decide. Six months earlier he wouldn’t have even considered it, but working together on his yard had meant she was at his place more than ever. Just the two of them eating meals and planning spaces.

The time together had only heightened his attraction to her, not just physically, but that connection of something more.

Or had it all been in his head? She didn't seem to feel it.

The thought of putting himself out there, or risking her kicking him to the curb, was a little terrifying, but he didn't know if he would be able to live with himself if he waited until it was too late.

When he returned home before dawn he was no closer to an answer about how to approach Adelyn, or even if he should try again, but at least he was tired enough to drop into a couple hours of real sleep before getting up for work.

Chapter Eighteen

Adelyn sat in the back of the library meeting room with Comfrey and Nick while Daniel talked to the women from the shelter program about small business loans. There were six women, most of whom had been to her presentation a few weeks earlier, but far fewer were here tonight. She supposed that entrepreneurial spirit wasn't for everyone—and that was okay. Running a business was a lot of work, and she knew that just getting through the day could be struggle enough for a lot of these women without adding the stress of starting a new business. Several of them had started on a very small scale, but getting a loan meant getting serious and taking on risk that might be beyond what they could handle in their current circumstances.

Still she wanted to encourage them to take those first steps toward their dreams, and learning about their options was an important one.

Daniel was interesting, vibrant, and charming as he talked about different ways to package a loan, the advantages and drawbacks of some business types depending on the kind of loan or grant they were looking for, and a few of the loans and grants he had researched that would apply specifically to women in their situations.

He fielded questions about different kinds of savings options—

regular savings versus bonds versus CDs. Adelyn was impressed with the questions they were asking, which showed how well-informed they were.

"I had a client come in this morning and bring me a thank-you basket for helping with their loan. It included this Lotto ticket." Daniel waved it for them to see. "I guess this is his idea of a good investment. I get that a lot of you have almost nothing left over at the end of the month, not because you aren't careful with your money, but because you struggle to keep food on the table. You'd be better off putting the money under a mattress, than *investing* in the lottery. You ladies are welcome to any winnings that come from it." He set it on the table and moved on.

A general chuckle ran through the room.

He moved on to the next topic and Adelyn had all but forgotten the ticket, until she saw several of the women talking afterward. They all took pictures of the numbers with their phones and Sheila—Felicia's babysitter—tucked the ticket into her purse, laughter on her face.

Adelyn watched the women interact with each other, Daniel, and Comfrey when the meeting was over.

Nick seemed to be staying out of their way when he sidled up to her. "He makes a good impression. Obviously he's good at his job. Did you meet him through work?"

"No, one of those internet dating sites. I got lucky, he's a good guy."

"Apparently it can be hard to recognize when you have something good. And even harder to hold onto it." He was looking at Comfrey, his mouth pursed a little with unhappiness.

Adelyn wished she could get Comfrey alone to pepper her with questions, but that wasn't going to happen tonight, so she set it aside for now. They did have the cake tasting with the other girls on Friday, maybe she could arrange to give Comfrey a ride.

Before she and Daniel took off that evening, Adelyn made certain to arrange it.

"So, where are we going for dessert?" Adelyn asked as she and Daniel headed out to his car.

Daniel took her hand as they exited the library. "I was thinking Sweet Confections, unless you have somewhere else you'd rather go?"

"No, I love that place. I never turn down a chance to go there."

"Perfect."

"I thought your presentation went really well. Thanks for coming. I know Comfrey appreciated it. She's one of several women who have tried to give the women at the shelter—and a number of those that are on their own now—the training and tools they need to succeed."

"I think it's great. I'm glad I could help. A few of the women are going to stop by this week for more details on the programs for the kind of businesses they want to open. But did you notice they still scooped up the Lotto ticket?"

"It was sitting there—you offered it to them for free. It's not like they spent their own money on it."

"Some people have to keep their eye on the main chance, even when it's about the longest shot there is." He stopped at his car and opened the side door for her. "Then again, using that singles website seemed like a serious long shot and it brought us together."

He moved closer to her, his fingers brushing along her neck as he rubbed his thumb down her chin, tipping her head back for better access to her mouth. Anticipation built as she slowly moved in, and their lips met. She felt that familiar flutter of pleasure in her chest, enjoyed the brush of his lips against hers and let the kiss linger for a long moment before pulling back. There were no rockets, but she certainly enjoyed the flutter.

"We don't get to do that often enough."

"No, we don't." She searched his face, wondering what was going through his mind. She glanced over at her car, which was parked a couple slots down. Maybe she should drive over so he wouldn't have to bring her back, but then he was helping her sit in his car and she let it go. He was so nice—why was she holding parts of herself back? Maybe they needed to move the conversation from texting to seeing each other in person more.

Sweet Confections was busy, as usual, and they waited in line to order before finally locating a table in the far corner. This new location on Indulgence Row had been good for them and she was happy to see the first few businesses to open up there were doing well.

"So how did you get involved with the women's shelter?" Daniel asked.

Adelyn talked about the garden and getting to know Comfrey, about how she'd talked with Charlee about her work there with the women and how impressed she had been with the program. "It's a great opportunity. Not all of the women at the shelter take advantage of it, but most of them do—and the ones who do tend to become independent faster and to be more successful on their own. Not always, but most of them have been battered by a boyfriend, husband, or other family member, and a lot of them have kids. The kids are the main reason most of the moms resorted to the shelter—they want so desperately to give their children a safe home and better future. How can you not want to be involved with something like that?"

He studied her face, their hands joined on the table. "You're a good woman, Adelyn. I'm glad I met you. I think this could really be something, you and me."

Before Adelyn could respond, a young woman brought them their desserts.

Adelyn was glad—she hadn't known how to respond—she liked him, a lot, but wasn't sure she was in the same place he was, not yet, anyway. When the server had gone, Adelyn changed the subject to his childhood. All she needed was more time to get to know him.

Chapter Nineteen

For the second time in one week Adelyn found herself at Sweet Confections. She had walked to work that morning so she would feel better about the extra calories tonight, but she would rather walk to work every day for a month than to miss this tasting.

Adelyn did manage to pick up Comfrey for the tasting, but didn't get a chance to ask about Nick since Comfrey talked non-stop about the plans several of the women had put together for their new businesses. Some of it seemed kind of pipe-dreamy to Adelyn. Even a very good loan would have to be paid back, and grants weren't exactly a dime a dozen, but she really hoped the women were able to make things happen. They had all been through too many disappointments and struggles already.

So, she put off the discussion about Nick until later.

Both brides had picked out their cake designs weeks earlier, but neither had settled on the flavors for the cake and filling. Sweet Confections had started holding big tastings for wedding cake customers every couple of months. Each person paid a fee to join, but the bride and groom's portions would come off the final cost of their cake. It made sense and was well worth the price for the chance to taste-test all the flavors.

She had known there would be other groups there, but hadn't

expected the whole bakery to basically be filled with customers for the tasting. Thankfully, Maddie was seated in the back at a large table—big enough that with a couple extra additions, they could fit the whole group of ladies, the two grooms, and two mothers. And was that Jason? It was good they were all such close friends, Adelyn thought as she squeezed into the booth, because there wasn't much room.

When Jason got out to let Reece sit beside Piper, he moved over to Adelyn's side, squeezing next to her. "I'm not sure if this is big enough for all of us."

"No kidding, but I don't know where else we would sit—the place is packed!"

The bakery owners and workers brought around platters with cake samples every ten minutes, changing the varieties and combinations so everyone would have a chance to test the different kinds. Even though the samples were tiny, Adelyn had eaten her fill before the final sample came around.

They passed the tray, but Adelyn waved it off. "No more, not unless you want me to explode."

"I'm done too," Piper said. "I know my preference."

"Oh yeah? What if I disagree?" Reece asked.

"You won't." His brows lifted, but he didn't say anything more as he tried another kind of cake.

"You girls have such delicate stomachs," Jason took another bite.

"It's how we keep our delicate figures," Adelyn said.

Jason groaned, chewing slowly. When he had swallowed he picked up another like it and held it out for her. "Seriously, that was amazing. You have to try this."

"They were all amazing," Adelyn protested.

"Come on, you'll think you died and went to heaven. You have to try it."

"It's not chocolate. I don't think you can describe anything not chocolate that way."

He looked into her eyes. "Trust me."

Adelyn still hesitated for a couple seconds before opening her mouth to take the cake he had poised just beyond her lips.

His fingertips brushed along her bottom lip as he pulled back after she took the bite—it was that touch as much as the exquisite perfection of the cake flavors that gave her chills.

She slowed her chewing to enjoy every moment of the creamy sweetness of the filling mixed with the spicy cake. Her eyes drifted closed so she could focus on the flavor. "You're right, that is heavenly. Can I order that every day or is it only for weddings?"

Everyone laughed and a couple people asked what she had eaten.

"Hazelnut almond with an Italian cream center," Jason read from the sticker on the plate.

Piper scribbled it in her notebook. "Now we know what kind to get when you get married."

"Are you getting married?" Jason's brows furrowed.

"Maybe someday, in the very, very distant future. But seriously, for my next birthday, that's the one."

Everyone chuckled and the brides and grooms settled on their cake and filling flavors.

It was high time, in Adelyn's opinion. Both weddings were less than a month away, and they still had to work out the details for the wedding dance Piper had agreed to last spring.

On the drive home Comfrey chatted about the upcoming Permaculture course she would be helping to teach until Adelyn pulled over on the street by the community garden.

"What are we stopping for?" Comfrey asked.

"You've talked about every subject possible except for the guy who clearly traveled across half the country to be here with you. I thought I'd pull over and let you talk yourself out until you realized you have no choice but to tell me about you and Nick. He's the one the matchmaker hooked you up with, isn't he? You didn't mention before that you were engaged."

Comfrey looked at Adelyn, then out the window, as if she were trying to decide if she would rather be walking home. Finally, though, she spoke. "Yes, we met through the match maker right after I finished college. I dated in college, but kept things casual, because I wanted to focus on my classes. Nick had been in a semi-serious relationship before me, but it had fizzled when they realized their dreams lay in totally opposite directions. Our mothers both pushed us to meet with the matchmaker, and she paired us up.

"We had chemistry from the start, a tight connection that grew so fast, faster than I had ever thought it could. Before I knew it, our mothers were the best of friends and our fathers were golfing buddies. I was working for my dad's cosmetics company and we were engaged in under a year. Our moms moved into wedding-planning mode in a frenzy."

"Wait, wait. I knew you had money, but Huxley Cosmetics?" Adelyn tried to wrap her head around that.

"That's the one."

"Processing." She might need to move processing to another day. "Okay, go back to Nick. Everyone was thrilled about the engagement."

"Over time everything seemed to crowd down on me until I realized I couldn't do it. I couldn't stay in that high-pressure, high-society lifestyle. My father rejected any idea I came up with out of hand and I wasn't happy with the products we were making. I had way too many social engagements I was required by my parents to attend.

"And I saw Nick digging into contract law at my father's company and enjoying it. He didn't necessarily relish the social scene the way some of our peers did, but he enjoyed it more than I did. I could see how it would go if we married, especially if we stayed in Boston, working for my father. I needed something different. You know I discovered permaculture in college while I was taking some landscaping classes—just for fun. It was interesting and challenging in a way that I hadn't felt about my business classes."

She sucked in a deep breath as though trying to decide what to say. "It wasn't that I didn't love Nick. I totally did, but as the wedding grew closer, I started having panic attacks. When I overheard our mothers planning the honeymoon, I realized I was done. The next day I returned Nick's ring with a note. I was a jerk and left them in his room instead of telling him to his face. I don't know if I could have left if I'd had to face him. I'm such a wimp."

"Seems like he's forgiven you. And that you still have chemistry," Adelyn said.

"Yes, but it doesn't change the fact that I can't live that kind of life. Visit it once in a while, but not live there all the time."

"So, you're not even going to give him a chance?"

Comfrey pursed her lips. "I'm dating Tony now. He's a great guy, and we're having such a terrific time together. How can I hurt him to give Nick a do-over? Especially when Nick isn't going to be around that long."

"Two amazing men to choose from. What a terrible situation to be in," Adelyn's voice was dripping in sarcasm.

"It is. But you should know. It's not like you don't have sparkage with two guys."

"I don't." As soon as she said it, Adelyn realized her protests had been perhaps a tad too quick.

"Give me a break, I saw you with Jason when he fed you that

cake. The sparks nearly knocked everyone else out. And then there's Daniel."

"You're totally wrong. Jason and I are—"

"Just friends," Comfrey chorused with her. "Whatever. If you believe that, then maybe it's time you took a closer look at what's between you."

Adelyn turned the key in the ignition and pulled onto the road.

"You can run, but you can't hide from the truth. And if you don't explore whatever might be between you, someday you're going to regret it. Trust me on this."

Adelyn didn't answer for a long moment. "If there are sparks, they're all coming from him. There's nothing on my side." She remembered the way the brush of his finger and thumb on her lips had affected her, but she wasn't going to screw up their friendship. She wasn't.

"You can't have sparks without both flint and steel. Steel alone doesn't create anything but noise."

In a moment, Adelyn pulled in front of Comfrey's cottage. "That would make me flint, and I'm pretty sure that's not who I am."

Comfrey touched her arm and gave it a quick squeeze. "That's what we all say sometimes. Thanks for the ride." She got out and shut the door behind her.

Adelyn waited until she saw Comfrey walking into her home before pulling back onto the road.

There was no way. Losing Jason completely would have to be worse than just being friends.

Chapter Twenty

"You'll never believe it," Maddie said as she joined Jason at the garden on Monday evening. "All I can say is that it's a good thing Felicia and I will mostly be on the same schedule when school starts again." She waved acknowledgment to Felicia, who looked anxiously at a friend from the neighborhood. Felicia ran over to join the other girl.

Jason stared at his sister. "You're babbling without making any sense. What won't I believe?"

"Sheila, she and some friends won the Lotto. I saw them on the news before coming over here."

"What? That's crazy. How much did they win?"

"More than seventeen million dollars." Maddie slid on her thin, green and pink flowered gardening gloves. "I imagine that will be the end of the daycare."

"What daycare?" Adelyn asked as she towed Daniel over to join them.

Maddie quickly explained what she had seen.

"No way." Adelyn whirled to Daniel. "Do you think they used your ticket?"

He blinked a couple times and sucked in a breath. "Well, if so, giving it away was the most generous gesture I've ever made." He looked a little sick at the idea.

Jason secretly gloated at the man's discomfort—even knowing he shouldn't.

Piper joined them from her car on the side of the road and took charge, assigning duties to everyone.

"Where are Comfrey and her new friend?" Adelyn asked after glancing around.

"I don't know about Nick, but Comfrey said she and Tony would be a few minutes late. I guess they stopped for dinner."

"Tony? Our Tony?" Jason couldn't see the two of them together—she was far too granola and Tony was a suit. Well, okay, he did know how to work power tools and wasn't afraid to get dirty, but it still seemed like an odd matchup. Sure, they had done the date things after the bachelor auction, but he thought it had ended there.

"Who else?" Adelyn shrugged and moved away with Daniel.

Ralphie joined the other kids and Maddie put them to work picking tomatoes.

"Things are really coming on now," Adelyn said.

"No kidding," Piper agreed. "The elementary school said they would take all the produce they could get their hands on once school starts, but that's a while away yet. We'll have to have a vegetable stand tomorrow morning. Comfrey said she would run it with some of the kids."

"Good. I don't think I can squeeze that into my schedule right now."

A few minutes later Tony's car pulled up with Comfrey in the passenger seat. She held a clipboard in one hand when he opened her door for her, and after talking to Maddie, Tony headed back to help the kids. Comfrey stayed to talk to Maddie for a little while before continuing what he understood had been a full day of trying to get people to sign her petition for a zoning variance.

Jason returned to work, though he couldn't help but glance Adelyn's direction and noticing the bags under her eyes and the way she sighed as she hauled a basket toward the green beans. He didn't say anything at first–he didn't want to tick her off by saying she looked bad. Especially since she didn't look bad, just a little more worn around the edges than usual.

He got to work pulling weeds a couple rows over, listening in while she and Daniel talked about paint colors for his house and whether he should go with a contrasting or complementary color for the trim. They talked about childcare, and speculated about what Sheila and her friends would be doing with their winnings, and whether or not they would take it in one lump sum, or spread it out over the decades.

The third time Adelyn yawned into her sleeve, Jason tossed the weeds he had just pulled into the bucket at the end of the row and approached. "Have you been having trouble sleeping? You seem tired."

"It's fine," she said, waving him off. "I've had a few late nights working on the wedding stuff but it's no big deal. You should see the decorations I've been putting together. They're going to be perfect."

"How late is late?" Jason asked as Adelyn covered yet another yawn.

She didn't answer at first, but by now Daniel was also staring at her as they waited for the answer. Finally she rolled her eyes though she managed to look irritated at being questioned. "It's been one or two in the morning the past few days. I had evening events and I needed to get through everything. Maddie's wedding is practically here."

"Tell me about it, but I don't think either of us want you killing yourself to make our weddings perfect. We can help," Piper protested.

"No, you have more than enough on your hands with everything else you need to do for the wedding. I'll be fine. I'm almost done with her stuff. A few more nights and yours will be done as well, then I can be perfectly rested for the weddings."

As if. Jason knew Adelyn wouldn't slow down—she'd probably push herself until she fell over from exhaustion. He walked over and took her by the hand, tugging until she stood up. "You go home and relax. Go to bed early. You're not going to do anyone any good if you get sick." He lifted the bucket of green beans she had been holding in her other hand.

"I'm fine. Give it back." Adelyn grabbed the other side of the handle and gave it a tug.

Jason stared at her, not relenting, waiting until she looked back up at him, fire flashing in her eyes. He lowered his voice to keep it gentle. "Sometimes you push yourself too hard and you need someone else to tell you that it's time to step back and take a break for your own good. This is one of those times."

Adelyn's mouth thinned for several second before her shoulders dropped. She nodded, and released the bucket. "You're right. I have been burning the candle at both ends. I'm pretty tired."

"Go home. Rest. We can handle this," Piper agreed.

"It'll give me more time to work on the decorations anyway."

"No, not tonight," Jason said. "Rest and bed."

"But once these are done I still have to put up lights all over your yard."

"I'll help with that. Better yet, I'll get someone to help *me*. You just stop by and show me where they need to go—tomorrow or the next day. Tonight, you rest and go to bed early."

He wasn't sure if she was going to do it at first, but when she nodded, he knew he could believe her. Still, he was going to drive by after they finished up here and make sure her lights were off.

Jason knelt with the basket of beans at the spot where Adelyn left off and got back to work.

"You two must be pretty close," Daniel said after several minutes of working alongside Jason. "How long have you known Adelyn again?"

"Practically since she was in diapers. She may be my sister's best friend, but we've been friends on our own for a long time too."

"Hmm." Daniel didn't say anything else, so Jason let it drop.

Daniel may not like Jason's friendship with Adelyn, but the feeling was mutual—especially since Jason intended to swap roles with the man.

One more item marked off Adelyn's list.

Chapter Twenty-one

Though she still had an enormous amount to do for the weddings, Adelyn had made a point of going to bed earlier the past several days and was feeling better, much to her embarrassment. That Jason had needed to point out the way she was wearing herself down was a great frustration. Why did she let herself get so overloaded? At least her mother had offered to handle the bridal showers–which Maddie and Piper had decided to do jointly. Her mother hadn't approved, but Adelyn had. She hoped that her mother would stick to the plan they had put together with the brides' input and not decide to "improve" it. Considering everything else Adelyn had to do for the wedding, not having to worry about the joint shower had saved her a lot of work. Besides, if Michele wanted to help, maybe this would be a chance for them to finally start to connect.

Adelyn walked up the front stairs Saturday morning an hour before the guests were scheduled to arrive in case her mother needed help with something. The first thing her mother did when she saw Adelyn was look her up and down to study her outfit.

"That's very nice," Michele said though the look in her eye didn't denote full approval. "Where did you get those shoes, JCPenney?"

Adelyn bit back her retort as she smiled at her mother. "Thanks for hosting the party, I really appreciate you taking the time." It was safer to ignore the question and move on.

"You know how I like to throw a party. It was fun putting it together, besides, I feel like I've raised those girls too. "

Adelyn couldn't argue that she, Piper, and Maddie had practically lived at each other's homes, but they hadn't spent that much time at Adelyn's house. Mostly, they had gone to Maddie's. It helped that Maddie's mom, Eve, had always welcomed them with open arms and frequently with homemade cookies.

"Well, I know that they appreciate you helping out like this. I do too, we've all been a little swamped, getting everything ready for the weddings on time."

"Well everything is perfect. I spent most of the last week working on this party."

They walked from the entry into the parlor area where the party would take place. The whole space was decked out in tasteful and elegant decor in cool blue and peach tones to suit both brides' color schemes. Food was already laid out on the banquet table along one side with chafing dishes set up to accept the things that were still warming in the oven. The tables held not just the elegant and sufficient tableware that her mom had always owned or party themed paper plates, but fancy stoneware she must have rented from a caterer. Adelyn had told her not to go to all of that extra expense, and that she would be more than happy to help with finger food and desserts, but Michele had gone overboard, as usual. At least the color schemes had been followed, and there was nothing too outlandish. She would have to see how many other changes Michele made to the plan Adelyn had created with her.

"It looks lovely, Mom. Thank you so much. I'm sure the party will be great." Adelyn set down the bag of pictures and other decorations she had brought to contribute to the shower. Over the past couple of weeks, she had started collecting snapshots of the two couples, both with her own camera, and from other friends and family members. She had also swiped several from the engagement photo sessions to display around the room.

“What are those?” Michele asked. "I thought you were leaving the decorations up to me."

Adelyn smiled, anticipating the question. "You've done a great job, but I wanted to add a personal touch to the party, and images of them with their fiancés seemed like the perfect addition to everything you've already done." She took several minutes to scatter the photos around.

Michele did not look happy about the additions, but she didn't argue either. That was a win in Adelyn's book. She was feeling self-congratulatory on having handled that without a confrontation. That was until she saw the food her mom had set out in the kitchen. Gone were the finger foods and pizza rolls the girls had requested, the fluffy icing-topped cupcakes Adelyn had shown her mom pictures of were nowhere to be found. Instead the oven held chafing dishes with rolls of vegetarian lasagna, mini quiches, and other fancy fixings that didn't fit the bill. On the table was an enormous, elaborate cake with the two couples’ names on it and two rather expensive-looking bride and groom sets that actually matched the couples. They were lovely, but not at all what they had discussed.

"It looks like you made some substitutions on the menu."

Michele smiled. "I know we discussed other food, but it just seemed so common. When I saw these options at the caterers, I knew they would be perfect. And look at this cake! It's practically perfect. They really should be using her to do their wedding cakes."

Adelyn ground her teeth and held her tongue. There was no point in making a huge issue about it now. What was done was done. Arguing with her mom had never helped anyway. "It is lovely.

Wait until you see the cakes they picked out at Sweet Confections, they're also very beautiful."

"I never trust people who compete in those cake shows. We all know those things are totally rigged. Just because they won something doesn't mean anything." Michele's nostrils flared slightly to show her displeasure that the other two brides had chosen differently than she would have if they had asked her opinion—she'd had four weddings of her own, so she must be the expert.

Adelyn tried to tone down the sarcasm in her own mind. Her mom was her mom and that wasn't going to change, so Adelyn would just focus on being thankful that she hadn't had to put together the entire party by herself. At least if she told herself that enough, she might be able to forget the variations her mom had introduced into their plan.

At least everything was very tasteful. Though her mother's style of doing things may not have matched the desires of the brides, she did know how to put together a classy party.

Piper and Maddie arrived moments after the first guests. Still, Adelyn heard her mother mutter something under her breath about how the guests of honor should have been there well before anyone else. Adelyn smiled through her irritation and greeted her two friends with large hugs. "Welcome to your party! Mom has been working very hard to make sure that it's everything you deserve."

"Everything is lovely, and I'm sure the food will be delicious," Maddie managed with only a slight uptick of her brow after she caught a look at the food.

Piper agreed and they were led to the seats of honor at a table near the buffet. Adelyn took coats, seated guests, and made introductions between the few people who didn't know everyone else at the party yet. Michele flitted around introducing herself to everyone and as the doorbell kept ringing even after Adelyn was sure that everyone must be there. She didn't know who some of these people were. There were others that she recognized but she was certain they hadn't been on the original guest list she'd given her mother.

Adelyn pulled her mother aside as soon as there was a break in the new arrivals. "Mom, I don't remember inviting the ladies sitting on the settee."

She patted her hair as if it was no big deal. "I invited a few extra people. It's not that big of a deal, they're very generous and they love bridal showers. Besides, they all know who Maddie's parents are, and everyone is happy to see Reece settling down finally."

"But they don't know the brides."

"Of course they do, do you think my friends would come to a party for someone they had never met? Now quit being such a bore and come join the party. It's going to be a lot of fun."

Adelyn looked across at her two friends and Piper shot her a curious glance. Adelyn shrugged and smiled in apology. Thankfully her friends were too gracious to say anything, despite having warned her of the impending problem.

"Oh look, it's your friend who wants to raise *goats in the city*." Mother's voice was just the other side of polite, making it obvious that she didn't approve of Comfrey.

Adelyn gritted her teeth. If her mother had only realized that Comfrey was the heir to Huxley Cosmetics, she would have done her best to ingratiate herself, whatever it took.

"Thank you for the invitation. I'm excited to be here." Comfrey passed over two gift bags for the brides.

"I'm sure you are."

Comfrey smiled like she hadn't been insulted—no doubt a highly refined talent. "I also have the party favors for the guests. I brought a few extra in case someone forgot to RSVP."

"That was a good idea. We have had a few of the family members show up unannounced. Thank you." Mom took the unassuming shipping box and slid it back beside one of the tables.

Michele had been correct that the unexpected guests were very generous, and joined in with gusto. They also were very imaginative about the honeymoon clothing they purchased for the new brides. Adelyn wondered if Piper's face would ever return to its normal complexion.

She hoped her two friends wouldn't kill her when this was all finished.

Thankfully the party ended on time, everyone adored the handmade soap and bath bomb favors Comfrey had assembled using products from Dierdre, one of the former shelter women Comfrey worked with. Finally everyone returned home leaving Adelyn with her mom, Piper, and Maddie. As soon as her mother went into the kitchen, leaving them alone, Maddie leaned over to Adelyn and whispered, "Who were those ladies?"

"I am so sorry," Adelyn rubbed her hands down her face. "I had no idea my mom was inviting extra guests. Of course you did get some rather nice gifts from them."

"Like I'll ever be able to wear any of those things," Piper said, mortified.

Maddie laughed. "Come on, Piper, they weren't that bad. Well, *some* of them weren't that bad. Maybe you'll get more adventurous after a while."

"You can't say that they didn't enjoy themselves. Or that they didn't provide plenty of entertainment for the rest of us," Adelyn said.

"Yeah, that's exactly what I was afraid of." Piper gave Adelyn's shoulder a small hug. "Just wait until it's your turn. The handcuffs are coming out."

"Whatever, and don't remind me. At least it should be a good long while before we have to even think about mine."

"So you say. You and Daniel sure seemed comfy the other day." Maddie asked.

"Don't get ahead of yourself–we've only been on a few dates."

“Six by my last count. That’s not a few anymore.”

“Maddie’s right, by the time I had been out with Reece six times I was mostly in love.”

“And I was in love with Ben way before that.” Maddie grinned nostalgically.

“You were in love with Ben in second grade, so that hardly counts. Now, you two go stash your loot at your places and get back to normal life. I need to swing by Jason's and count up how many more packages of twinkle lights I need to track down for your weddings. I’ll see you both on Tuesday for dance practice." Maddie had picked the music and choreographed the dance–not they all had to learn it.

"You’re not leaving before you help me in here," her mom called from the kitchen.

"Of course not, Mom. I wouldn't dream of leaving before everything is cleaned up."

Adelyn helped Maddie and Piper out to their cars with their many boxes of gifts, and then returned to the house to wash dishes and clear tables.

"Thank you for putting together this party. I do appreciate it." Even though it hadn’t turned out quite the way she had anticipated, at least everyone had fun, there was plenty of food, and what else really mattered?

"It was a good time," Michele said. "We should do this kind of thing together more often. Have you ever thought about starting a wedding planning business? We could be the best." She nudged Adelyn with an elbow.

Adelyn wasn't sure that any bride would be completely thrilled with her mom basically planning the whole thing and ignoring input that the bride had given her but she chose to keep that to herself. "Too bad my job keeps me so busy. But the decorations were lovely, and the food was delicious as always. I can't believe Maddie's wedding is only a week away."

"Well, it sounds like you've been busy with all of the landscaping projects out at that McCormick boy's house. Are you sure there's nothing going on between the two of you?"

"He's not the one I'm dating."

"You keep saying that, but I still haven't met this mysterious man. Don't you think it's time you brought him by for Sunday dinner so we can meet him and see if he's good enough for you?"

Adelyn wanted to shudder at the very suggestion. She was not going to parade Daniel and his son around in front of her Michele and Clark so they could find fault. "You'll meet them when you meet them." *And not until I'm ready.* "Besides we haven't been dating that long."

"Long enough that Marianne mentioned seeing you two together. And you know how people start to talk. It's not right that I'm going to be the last person to meet this man."

Her mother had a point. On the other hand, Adelyn wasn't ready to have this turned into a nightmarish let's-plan-your-wedding scenario. So, it would have to wait a little while. "I promise you'll meet him soon enough. In the meantime, you'll have to be happy knowing that I'm finally dating someone and he's very nice, and he has a steady job, and that should be enough for you."

"Of course. Why should I expect to be included in the important parts of my daughter's life? I'm just happy knowing that you're dating someone. What mother really expects her daughter to introduce her to the man she's dating before he's ready to pop the question? I mean he lives all the way across town. It must take you at least ten minutes to get from his house to this one."

Knowing she was in the wrong, but not ready to change the status quo, Adelyn changed the subject. "So where is Clark today? Did he decide to hide out considering all of the women descending on his house?"

Michele gave her the stink eye but, she allowed this change of subject. Hallelujah! They spent the last ten minutes of cleanup time discussing Clark's job, her mother's vacation plans the next month, and the plans for the weddings.

When Adelyn finally left, she was very grateful to have the event over with, and that she hadn't been roped into bringing Daniel and his son to dinner yet.

She had a little more wiggle room before she absolutely had to let those two parts of her life meet.

Chapter Twenty-two

Jason came home with another load of supplies from the home improvement store to finish up some projects in the kitchen. Between working on the house to get ready for the weddings, the yard work with Adelyn, and preparing the final paperwork for the house that he was going to be building, he hadn't had a lot of free time to relax lately, and he was looking forward to getting the first wedding over with.

He hadn't expected to come home to find Adelyn walking through his backyard looking as pressed and pretty as if she had just gotten off work. She stood scribbling something in her notebook, standing between the pergola and the vine-covered trellis. Finding her in his yard, at his home, when he came home felt so right. He left everything he had purchased in the truck and stepped onto the grass, crossing over to her.

She was focused on the newly completed yard and hadn't appeared to notice him yet. This gave him an extra moment to watch her and the way the hot evening breeze blew the hairs against her face and ruffled the papers in her notebook. The scent of blooming flowers wafted toward him on the breeze, swirling and whirling in the hot air. When she looked up his heart nearly fell at his feet.

She was everything he had ever wanted.

"Hey, I expected you to be home when I headed over. When you didn't answer the door, I came around back. I swung by to make sure I was going to get enough lights for the weddings. I've gone through mine, Piper's and Maddie's, but we'll need more. Do you have some we can put up? Otherwise I'll need to order some more tomorrow if I can't track enough down." Adelyn seemed totally unaware of the epiphany that was running through him. Sure, he had known that he cared about her, had thought he might love her, but this was something more. Something he couldn't put off any longer.

Jason reached out and took her hand in his, twining their fingers together. "I have a few. You wanna come in and check them out? I could make some coffee or tea."

Adelyn chuckled. "My mom fed us so much food at the bridal shower, I don't think I could eat another thing. But I'm almost done here and then I'll come in to look at the lights that you have in storage."

"Walk me through it," Jason said. "What are you covering with lights? What do you imagine the flow is going to be?" He had gone with what she wanted so far, liking her plans when he looked at his life in the house, but only getting bits of her plans for the weddings.

He held her hand as they walked around the backyard and she described it all to him. She didn't seem to notice that they were holding hands—or maybe she was enjoying it as much as he was. Basically, it sounded like she planned to cover nearly everything in twinkle lights. He was surprised she hadn't already bought three cases of them.

"So is Reece planning to kick in for my crazy electric bill this month?" he asked.

Adelyn grinned at him. "He may do that. But considering everything else he's bankrolling, maybe you need to hit up Ben instead."

Jason nodded, though he wouldn't—it was only two days, so it wouldn't be that much. "I'll keep that in mind." They headed back to the house and walked into the kitchen. He had taken her suggestion to keep some of the existing structures and refinished them instead of replacing them. The island got new stain and varnish, matching cabinet doors, and a new counter top. He had pulled out the other cabinets completely and was rebuilding them to his own specifications. The counter top for those was waiting in the garage for him to install. It was going to be tight if he wanted to get the kitchen done before the wedding, but he knew he could manage it. Sleep was optional, wasn't it?

"So would you like some tea?" he asked. "Or do you just want to get started on those Christmas lights?"

"I'll take some tea, thanks. Where are the Christmas decorations? I can pull them out while you're heating the water."

Since they were easy to access, he gave her directions, and put the kettle on the stove. Normally, he was more of a coffee guy, but not at this time of night. Besides, he knew she preferred tea. He tried to think about the next day and what was coming on the final project they were finishing up for Charlee, but his mind kept drifting back to the woman upstairs; he could hear her walking around the spare room. He missed having people in the house with him. His Army buddy Bo and Bo's wife Tosca had stayed with him for several weeks the previous fall. Ever since they had returned to Colorado, Jason had felt very alone in his own home.

Adelyn came down the stairs, her hands filled with several rolls of Christmas lights. "Do you mind if I plug these in to check them?"

"No, of course not. Go ahead. The outlet under the window is working now."

Adelyn tested each of the balls in turn and he tried not to focus too much on the pleasing visual she gave him when she leaned over.

Tried but failed. He turned his face away when the kettle started to squeal and filled two cups. "My mom left several varieties of tea in the cupboards not too long ago. Do you have a preference?"

"Do you have orange spice? If not, I like peppermint." Adelyn chatted about several things she was preparing for the yard, hinting at the surprise the girls had for Reece, and the last few things she needed to do before the wedding rehearsal, which was only days away. She managed to keep her griping about her mom's changes to the bridal showers to only two short comments, then focused on how well everything else had gone.

It felt so right having her there in his kitchen talking through their plans and their day. Jason didn't want it to end. As they sat sipping their cups of tea, she met his gaze and something passed between them, something in her gaze that he hadn't seen before. Did she feel the attraction too? Was he wrong about not saying anything to her about it before? Their fingers brushed just as they had at the cake tasting, and he couldn't help himself. He had been waiting too long already.

"How are things going with that guy you're seeing?" Jason asked. "It seems like he's pretty into you."

"They're good. I enjoy spending time with him." She glanced down at her hands.

His heart pounded and his hands started to sweat, but he had to say it, even if she didn't want to hear it. He sucked in a breath. "I can understand that, him really being into you, because I've felt that way myself for a very long time."

Her eyes, which had drifted away at the mention of Daniel, now swiveled back to his. "What do you mean?"

For a second he was tempted to back pedal, but he couldn't. Not again. Not after all the times he had to let things go when he had known what he wanted to say. "Adelyn, we've been friends for a really long time. Sure, at first we were just buddies, I was Maddie's older brother, and that was it. But since I returned from Afghanistan, I haven't only seen you as Maddie's best friend."

Adelyn sat straighter, shifting away from him. She had refused to ask him what he meant at the fair, but not this time. "What do you mean?"

"I'm in love with you, Adelyn. I've been trying to fight it for a long time, but it's not working."

"I'm . . . dating Daniel. How could you say this to me now? *Now*, when I'm dating Daniel?"

"I know the timing is terrible, but I can't keep it all inside anymore. I had to tell you. Spending all of this extra time with you has made it even more obvious to me that we're perfect together."

Adelyn set down the cup she had been holding for the last minute without having sipped out of it. "I'm sorry, Jason, you're a great guy, really great. And I like you so much, but I'm dating Daniel."

"Yeah, you mentioned that. But think for a minute–how well does he complete your list? Then think about how well I complete your list."

Her mouth worked for a few seconds. "I don't care about the list anymore, and anyway, they're just guidelines, not a hard-and-fast rule. I decided it wasn't doing me any good, having such unreasonable expectations."

"There's a reason you made the list–and you know you need the things on it."

"I have to go." She jumped up from her seat and all but dashed for the back door, leaving it slightly open in her wake.

Jason wanted to chase her down to stop her and tell her she was making a mistake. But his heart was aching far too much for that.

How had he screwed that up so completely? Her feelings for him were nothing. Apparently.

This is why he had kept his feelings to himself for so long. Was there any way to make her reconsider?

Adelyn hurried to her car not knowing what to think. She had been so sure that Jason didn't see her as anything but a friend, that she hadn't listened when everyone said he liked her. He was an awesome guy, a great friend, but she *did* have Daniel.

What did Jason think was going happen anyway? Did he think she would leave the guy she was with to be with someone else—the way her father had done time and again? Did he really think she was that kind of woman?

And why hadn't she handled it all as if it wasn't a big deal, instead of turning it into one? Would this ruin their friendship? She got into her car and pulled out of the driveway, looking back to see him glancing at her through his front window. She should go home. Just go home and put it all behind her, and pretend it never happened.

He said he loved her. Love, not like.

She couldn't just go home and not talk through it with somebody. Could she discuss it with Maddie? Would it be way too weird and put her in the middle? Piper might be a better choice. Adelyn dialed Piper's phone while she sat at the red light and waited for the call to come through her stereo system.

"Hello."

"Hi, Piper, do you have a few minutes so I can talk to you?"

"I'm sorry, I'm not at home. Reece had a business dinner he had to go to and he brought me along. We were about to go in. Is something wrong?"

"No, no, it's fine." Adelyn didn't want to distract Piper if she was going to a business thing. She knew how those dinners stressed out her friend. "It can wait until later. Have fun at your dinner." She hung up as she passed the community garden.

Comfrey.

At the next corner, she did a U-turn and headed back in the direction she'd come from, diverting down Comfrey's street. Thankfully, Comfrey's car was parked out front, and no one else's was. Hopefully, that meant Comfrey was home alone.

Adelyn sighed in relief when Comfrey opened the door a minute later, and invited her in.

"Hi, Adelyn, what's going on? I was just going to go down to my property to check on the goats." She looked at Adelyn a little closer. "Are you okay?"

"Yeah. Sort of."

Comfrey's eyebrows lifted and she grabbed Adelyn by the arm, towing her over to the sofa. "You don't look okay. What's going on?"

Grateful for a listening ear, Adelyn opened up and told Comfrey about the conversation she had just had with Jason. "I can't believe you were right. I honestly didn't believe it. Or didn't want to believe it."

Comfrey grinned. "Never doubt me. Besides, he's not that good at hiding it. You should see the way he moons over you when he thinks you're not looking."

Adelyn covered her face. "Moons over me?"

"Well maybe that's taking it a little far," Comfrey admitted. "But it's pretty obvious that he's totally into you. What are you going to do about it?"

Adelyn had no idea. "I was kinda hoping you would have some suggestions. I can't believe I ran out of there like a scaredy-cat. We've been friends for so long."

"Well, how are things going with Daniel? What were you thinking about your relationship with him before today?"

Adelyn slumped in her seat. “I like him. He’s a terrific guy, and a great kisser. But I’m not sure that we have a future. That makes me feel bad, especially when I’m using him as the excuse for why I can’t go there with Jason."

"Well, I think you owe it to yourself to find out where your relationship with Daniel is going, without worrying about Jason's feelings. I think Jason is terrific, and I really hope things work out for the two of you, but if you aren’t sure that things with Daniel are definitely over, then you might look back and wonder *what if.* I don’t want that for any of you."

That was the direction Adelyn had been leaning. "I'm afraid that all of this is going to ruin my relationship with Jason. We've been friends for so long."

Comfrey shot her a commiserating look. "If your friendship has lasted this long, I'm sure it’ll last long enough for you to figure out how you feel about Daniel. If things with Jason are meant to be, you'll figure it out. Just focus on the relationship you’re already in first. Consider the relationship honestly on its own merit. If Daniel is the one for you, you’ll figure *that* out soon enough. If he’s not, you’ll see it so you can let him go. Jason has waited for you this long, I’m sure he’ll still be available in a week or two. If not, you can rescue your friendship, if you both want it enough."

She had shut him down and run away. She hoped Comfrey was right about Jason. She would hate it if everything went wrong from here on out. On the other hand, she wasn’t going to walk out on Daniel and the best relationship she’d ever had because there was a chance of something else that might or might not be better.

Feeling marginally better, Adelyn stood. "I should let you get back to what you're doing. Thanks for talking over everything with me. I couldn't call Maddie to talk to her about her brother."

"I understand. Hey, would you like to come out to the farm with me? My goats are adorable and could be a great distraction. The sheep are fun too." Comfrey stood.

Adelyn thought that sounded like a nice change of pace. "Sure, and I have more sensible shoes in my car. You never know when you might need some."

"You're a regular Girl Scout." Comfrey grinned. "Grab those shoes; I need to get the milking equipment. Have you ever milked a goat before?"

Adelyn laughed. "No, I haven't. Has anyone else you've taken out to milk with you done it before?"

"Not so far. But you surprise me sometimes." Comfrey picked up a bucket with several pieces of equipment in it and headed for the front door. "Hopefully the girls will behave for us today."

Either way, Adelyn felt pretty good about having a change of scene and something to distract her. Those wedding favors sitting on her dining table would still be there when she got home.

Chapter Twenty-three

Jason had stayed late at work Wednesday night knowing Adelyn, Maddie, Piper, and several others would be at his house stringing lights for the weddings. Wanting to take advantage of the excavator's one-day rental was a handy excuse.

It had been four days since he had told Adelyn that he loved her. At the moment he was having a hard time remembering exactly what he had said to her besides that. In any case, she had not been interested. He knew the wedding would have them together for much of the weekend, and he didn't want to stay away for so long that it became even more uncomfortable when they saw each other again, but a couple extra days wouldn't hurt.

Okay, he was being a total wuss—it was his house for crying out loud. There was no reason why he shouldn't be there, so when he finished digging the hole, he decided to man up and go help with the lights rather than finding something else to do for a while.

There were five extra cars parked along the street in front of his house that didn't belong to his neighbors. Even better—the larger the group, the less pressure he would have to talk to Adelyn.

The clouds were threatening rain, but it was only supposed to sprinkle, so everyone seemed determined to get the lights up while the weather was still cooperating. He hoped the weatherman was right about clear skies Friday and Saturday—Kansas weather could be incredibly unpredictable. Voices echoed from his backyard.

Ben's truck pulled into the driveway right behind Jason's and he was relieved to see his best friend would be there. How could he have been such a stupid idiot to go with his gut, telling Adelyn like that? He knew she was involved with someone else, why had he thought that she would just jump into his arms?

Then again, at least he knew now.

"Long day at work?" Ben joined Jason on the driveway.

"That's how it goes when you're starting your own business." It wasn't much of an excuse, since he had deliberately planned the project timing to coincide with the decorating party.

"Considering the pictures Maddie has been sending me for the past hour, they're probably almost finished. We appreciate you letting us take over your yard like this."

"Of course, you're my best friend."

"And, she's your sister."

"Well there is that, yes. I really haven't minded." At least not until lately.

Ben waggled his eyebrows. "I bet you haven't minded. How are things with you and Adelyn?" He opened the door to the house, walking into the empty living room. They could see people bustling around the backyard through the kitchen window. Front and center, of course, was Adelyn. Daniel was by her side.

This was going to be in no way awkward, Jason thought wryly to himself. "You might as well ask how things are going with Adelyn and Daniel."

"I didn't get the feeling that they were very serious. Am I wrong?"

"I don't know but...I told her the other day about how I felt about her, and she wasn't interested. She just reminded me she was seeing Daniel and took off like a scared rabbit."

"Wow, I can't believe you finally told her. I can't believe you waited until *now* to tell her."

“No kidding. My timing has never been so bad before."

"Well, at least now she knows. If things don't work out with her and Daniel, maybe something will work out with the two of you.”

Jason didn’t feel better about that. "Right, because I want to be second-place."

"That doesn't make you second place," Ben said. "If things don't work out with him but they do work out with you, then you’re first place. Be patient and see what happens."

Easier said than done.

Thankfully, Jason got sucked into decorating the moment he walked out the back door, so there wasn't any time to be uncomfortable with Adelyn. Especially since she was on the other side of the yard. Though he was always aware of her and where she was and what she was doing, Jason managed to relax after a little while, and when she finally did get close enough to talk to, things weren't nearly as weird as he had expected.

"Darla is really excited about her house," Adelyn said.

"I dug the foundation today. We’ll be pouring it next week.”

“That soon?” Adelyn asked

"Once we got the go-ahead from the city, we were golden."

“That's great, I'm excited for you."

"Thanks."

Several of the helpers had already taken off when it started to sprinkle. Adelyn and Daniel took off a few minutes later, with Reece and Piper hard on their heels. Jason expected Ben and Maddie to follow suit, but when he finished the string of lights he was working on, he looked up to find them standing in his kitchen talking. He wondered if Ben was telling her about things with Adelyn. Maybe Adelyn already had. If so, Maddie was being unusually quiet about it. Jason knew it was inevitable, and honestly he didn't even mind that much if she knew; he and Maddie had always been close.

He just wasn't sure if he wanted to deal with it right now. The rain strengthened and Jason hurried into the house before he was soaked.

"Your yard looks great," Maddie said when he entered. "I appreciate how hard you worked to make it happen this year."

"Thanks. I was glad to do it. Only a few more days until the wedding," Jason gestured to Ben with his thumb. "Then you'll be stuck with this guy forever."

Maddie put her arms around Ben's waist and looked up at him, smiling. "Works for me."

Ben leaned the few inches between them to kiss her.

"Do you have to go pick up Felicia from her aunt and uncle's house?" Jason asked. "Or are they bringing her back for the wedding?"

"They're bringing her back." Ben said. "They'll be here tomorrow afternoon, stay for the wedding, and then keep her at their place while we're on our honeymoon."

"I bet she's sad to have missed all of the pre-wedding planning." Jason took one of the cookies someone had brought to share with the helpers. "It's been kind of quiet without her around."

"It's amazing how quickly I got used to having her in my house." Ben had been his niece's guardian for less than six months.

"Some people worm their way into your life like that," Jason said.

Maddie's eyebrows lifted. "Is there something I don't know?"

Jason reached out and smudged a little dirt on her cheek as if wiping it away. "Nothing important."

Ben shot him a look that said volumes in sympathy. "We probably ought to head out, unless you'd like some extra company."

Jason shook his head. "You two take off. I need a shower and some dinner. I'll talk to you tomorrow."

Ben and Maddie left Jason in the suddenly echoing house. Yeah, he understood exactly what Ben meant. The only difference was that Adelyn had never lived with him like Felicia did with Ben.

He would have to get used to the idea that nothing would change between them.

Chapter Twenty-four

After spending the evening setting up chairs and tables in Jason's backyard the night before, Adelyn was relieved to see that everything still looked okay when she arrived five hours before the wedding Saturday morning. There had been more wind the previous night than they had banked on, but either it hadn't done any damage, or Jason had already cleaned things up. The plants and lights were all in place, the centerpieces were complete, and all of the guest favors were waiting in a box in her car.

However, there was still plenty to do.

Piper met her at the house to put on the table cloths and set out the centerpieces for the reception which would immediately follow the ceremony. While they messed with all of the little final details of decorating, Piper talked about a couple of minor adjustments she'd like to make to her own plans for her wedding the next weekend. Adelyn made an occasional note on the notepad she had brought with her containing the list of things that still needed to be done that morning. She still couldn't believe both of her best friends were getting married within a week of each other, and she wasn't even serious with a guy.

Not that things weren't going well with Daniel, the two of them had a lot in common and enjoyed their time together. For some reason however, she was having a difficult time feeling connected to him.

She put the last centerpiece on the table and then heard a knock coming from the house. She glanced over to see Jason standing in the windows of his barely finished kitchen holding a coffee pot and gesturing to Piper and herself. She gave him a wave of acknowledgment, and then returned to the empty box that had held the decorations. "Looks like Jason is inviting us in for a break," she said to Piper.

"I could use a pick-me-up. I can't believe we've already been at this for two hours."

"I think we're about done here. Which is good, since Maddie should be arriving to get ready any minute. We should follow suit."

They took the last of the empty cartons and packages into the house with them and picked up the cups of coffee that Jason had poured for them. Feeling awkward, Adelyn looked around the room, then gestured. "I can't believe you actually finished this in time. I was starting to wonder if you'd manage it."

"Me too. I was assembling and installing cupboard doors until two a.m. The door and drawer pulls still need to be added, and the crown molding on top but it's definitely all functional."

"It's beautiful, that's what it is. You've outdone yourself." Adelyn ran her hand along the cherry cabinet fronts. They were even better than she had imagined.

The front door opened and Maddie called out, "Hello, the blushing bride is here."

"Thanks for the coffee," Adelyn smiled at Jason before taking her cup to the front to greet Maddie. Piper echoed the thanks and the women disappeared upstairs to the guest room that had been designated at the bride's room.

Jason could still hardly believe that his sister was getting married that day. It seemed like only yesterday that she was eleven years old and in pig tails. The fact that it was his best friend marrying her did make that a little easier, but it was still a little weird sometimes. He was happy for them though—they were so happy together and Maddie was excellent with Ben's niece Felicia. Not that anyone was surprised by that—she was one of the favorite teachers at the elementary school across from the community garden.

He still had some preparations of his own to do that morning before the wedding. Beyond the physical efforts of greeting people, he needed to figure out how to move on from Adelyn, since it was obviously not going to work out. Luckily for him, Maddie had invited a couple of her old college roommates to the wedding, and had set him up with one of them. He had seen Leslie's picture a couple days ago, and remembered meeting her when she had been living with Maddie at college. He had liked Leslie, and hoped they would have a good time together. Maybe focusing on another woman would help him enjoy the day more.

Time to go get dressed before things started to get crazy.

Though Jason had been looking forward to seeing his baby sister again, he had not expected her to come with a boyfriend or half a dozen henna tattoos scrawled across her arm. It was a good thing Maddie wasn't one of those controlling, freak-out brides, or she might have wigged about all the wedding photos with her sister who had temporarily marked herself up in the most blatant way possible before the occasion. He wished he understood Angelina a little better sometimes. Despite their age difference they had been close once. It seemed like since she had gone off to New York to pursue acting, she had pulled even further away from the family, and he missed the sweet girl she used to be. Not that he expected her to stay the same, but she didn't seem happy and he wished he could help.

Angelina approached him on the grass after the wedding ceremony and slid an arm behind his back and around his waist. "It seems like forever since we talked last. What've you been up to lately, big brother?"

"Well, I'm starting my own business. I've finally finished getting my contractor's license and my first house build broke ground a few days ago. Plus, as you can see, the house here is keeping me busy."

"Yeah, it looks great. I can't believe what you've done with the kitchen. You know what it could use—drawer pulls would be really handy."

"Good idea. If you open the first drawer to the right of the sink, you'll see the ones I picked out already. You'll have to let me know what you think. How are things on the acting front?" He figured that if she had landed anything big he would have heard about it from his mom. Still, it didn't hurt to ask.

"Another spot in the chorus line. At least this one qualifies as off-Broadway and not out in the Bronx. And the script looks good. I was lucky to be able to get a couple of days off to come home for the wedding, my director rules with an iron fist."

"You still like it?"

"Yes, I love the acting. I'd just like a little more of it and a little less singing in the background. But, I take what I can get. Did you meet my boyfriend?"

If Angelina's appearance had momentarily surprised Jason, the boyfriend's appearance was even more unusual for their little town.

He had at least a dozen piercings and a shock of bright purple hair. Not that those things counted, but it seemed out of character for his sister who had once been such a straight shooter. "I haven't met him, but I saw him when you arrived."

"I was going to bring him over last night," Angelina said, "But we got in so late, I didn't want to bother you."

"You got in after two?" Jason asked. "Because that's when I went to bed."

"Wow, that's super late for you. I didn't expect you to still be up after eleven. If I'd known, I would've brought him over for you to meet."

"We probably would've stayed up even later if you'd come, and we have all weekend to catch up." It wasn't long enough, but he would take what he could get.

Angelina nodded as though she weren't completely convinced and Jason hoped there wasn't something more going on than he'd realized. He would have to look into that a little more later—after he dealt with whatever it was that Reece was waving him over for. He hoped there wasn't a problem in the house. Then he needed to get back to his date.

Adelyn tried her best to act normal around Jason at the wedding. She had managed to pretend that nothing had changed between them when they spoke, but things *had* changed, and she wasn't sure how she felt about it. He sure looked good in a tux, and she couldn't help but notice how friendly he was getting with Maddie's old roommate. She even caught herself thinking bad thoughts about the woman whom she had always liked before.

She was *not* jealous, though. She simply wanted the best for him.

Daniel took her hand, drawing her attention his way. "Hey, your mind seems to be wandering a lot tonight. What's going on?"

Adelyn smiled. "I can't believe how well everything went today. I expected something to blow up on me this morning, but it didn't."

"It all looks amazing," Daniel said. "You all have done a fantastic job of putting this together. Have you been planning this for a few years?"

"A few months actually." Adelyn laughed, "I knew this yard would end up perfect. You should have seen it in the spring, though."

"It's handy that Maddie's brother was able to host the wedding like this."

"Yes it is. And that he's willing to take suggestions." Adelyn thought of the many hours they had spent together planning the yard, preparing the beds, planting and maintaining it all over the summer. It had been a lot of work, but also a lot of fun. She had seen new sides to Jason that she'd never noticed before. It was funny how she could have known him for so many years and still not have seen him clearly. Why was that? Had she just not been looking? Or had he changed so much during that last deployment? She figured it was probably some of each.

She glanced over to see Jason lead Leslie onto the makeshift dance area they had set up for the night. It was in the grass, but plenty of people were still taking advantage of it. He twirled her around under his arm, and she laughed as she came into his embrace. Irritation shot through Adelyn. *This is stupid. I've got to stop this. I don't want him, so why am I annoyed at her?*

Except she was starting to think that maybe she did want him.

Jason chuckled at the puns Leslie was throwing his way. She was such a nice girl, and he was having fun with her. He twirled her around again and glanced over in time to see Adelyn snuggling up to Daniel. He looked away—he was not going to drive himself crazy watching them all night. He had a beautiful, funny woman in his arms, and he would do his best to focus on her for the evening. Maddie and Ben were dancing a few feet away and he smiled, he loved seeing them together.

Everything had gone so well, almost flawlessly. Felicia ran over to join the newlyweds and Maddie and Ben separated on one side, each taking one of her hands so they could dance as a trio. Yeah, things were going to be all right for them.

Leslie said something else, trying to draw Jason's attention, and he realized he'd missed the first half of her phrase.

"They look happy, don't they?"

"Yes, they sure do. They deserve it. I'm glad this whole thing has gone off without a hitch."

"Maddie told me how much work you put into getting the yard ready. It sounds like it was a huge task. You're a great brother."

"The landscaping needed to be done anyway, and hey, Reece ended up footing half the bill. Bonus for me."

"It does help to have a wealthy partner in the project," Leslie said.

"Yes, it does. And I had a lot of help with the actual work." He couldn't help but let his eyes drift back to Adelyn.

"I heard that Adelyn helped you with a lot of this. Maddie seems to think that the whole thing wouldn't have turned out nearly as well without her. Was she really that much help?"

Jason glanced over at Adelyn and Daniel again. "Yeah, she really was. It wouldn't have happened without her." She had made the difference in so many ways.

Who was he fooling? There's no way he was going to get over Adelyn anytime soon.

The bride and groom left about nine o'clock, heading straight for the airport for their midnight flight. Jason waved them off and then shook hands, said good night, and generally made his way around the crowd as they started to depart. Within twenty minutes ninety-percent of the people had left with only his parents, Ben's mom, Reece, Piper, and Adelyn left behind. They began stacking up all decorations, and putting things back to normal. There would still be things to finish up in the morning, but there were a lot of details that needed to be cleaned up before they left for the night.

"It was a beautiful evening," Adelyn said.

"Yes, it was. You did a great job with the decorations," Jason said.

"You seem to get along well with Maddie's roommate. Have you met her before?"

"Yeah, several times, but it's been years. This is the first time I've had a real conversation with her, though." Jason felt embarrassed talking to Adelyn about other women, especially now that she knew how he felt. He smiled and did his best to shrug it off. "What happened to Daniel? Did he take off already?"

"Yes, his babysitter had to go home." Adelyn focused on the center pieces she had in her hands as she carefully repacked them into a box.

"How old is his son?"

"Four. He's a little small for his age though, so he looks younger than that."

Eve came over with tablecloths folded in her arms. "Well, it's been a long day. You did a great job, you guys."

"Thanks, Mom." Jason took the cloths and stacked them with the others to be washed.

"I appreciate you saying so," Adelyn said. "It was a labor of love. Besides, we get to do this all over again next week. Jason, maybe you should consider renting your backyard out now that it's all finished."

Jason shook his head. "No way, this has been a lot of work. I just know if we rented the yard to other people, they would expect me to do all of the setup and cleanup. I'm starting a new business. What makes you think I have time for a second one?"

Adelyn laughed. "You've got me there. Anyway, I hope your grass semi-recovers before next weekend."

Jason looked across the grass, which had been growing in thicker and healthier all summer. It was starting to look pretty worn after all the people who had been trampling it that afternoon and evening. Maybe if they stayed off of it all week it would rebound before the big herd of feet crossed it again the next Saturday.

"I think this is the end of it," Ben's mom said as she came over with a few more tablecloths in her arms. "At least for now. It's been quite a night."

"Yes, it has. But a good one." Eve yawned–it was way past her normal bedtime.

Jason smiled, beyond ready for his own bed after the late night before. "Thanks for helping with the cleanup. That would have taken me ages."

"We'll help you clean up these tables and chairs tomorrow." His father joined them with Piper and Reece hot on his heels.

"I have some ideas for adjustments for next week," Piper said.

Jason groaned audibly, mostly out of teasing. "That's all Adelyn's department."

"No problem. Come help us finish cleaning up in the morning and we can sit down and discuss little changes afterward." Adelyn was always good at encouraging extra help for a project–not that Reece and Piper wouldn't have come anyway.

"We'll do that," Reece said. "Although, you did a fantastic job with this tonight. So if the changes Piper has in mind aren't going to work when the wedding is so close, don't worry about it."

"That's what he says." Piper gave Reece a little nudge in the ribs with her elbow, making him grin.

Her little brother Spencer, who had just turned fifteen, approached carrying a box with table centerpieces. "Good party. Can we go now?"

Piper smiled. "You betcha kid. Come on, let's get to bed."

"That's our cue," Reece said. "See you guys around one?"

Adelyn nodded. "One sounds perfect. Everyone should take it easy tomorrow morning."

Jason loaded the box of centerpieces into the back seat of Adelyn's car, after saying goodnight to everyone else, then headed back inside. The place was a total mess. He didn't have the energy left to clean it up tonight, so he would deal with it tomorrow. He went around to make sure the windows and doors were all locked, then went to bed.

With any luck he would be too tired to lay awake remembering how Adelyn had looked with Daniel on the dance floor.

Chapter Twenty-five

Adelyn hadn't seen Jason once since their Sunday cleanup party after Maddie's wedding. It had been thirteen days since he had told her he had fallen in love with her, and she still couldn't reconcile how she felt in her head with her heart.

Nor could she forget his comment about the list being important to her. It wasn't like Daniel didn't tick several of the boxes—important boxes. Just because he didn't tick them all didn't mean that he wasn't a good fit for her. They got along well, and his kisses were very nice, indeed.

So why did Jason's question about how well Daniel fit her list keep playing in her head over and over? She was giving things with Daniel her best effort, but the harder she tried, the less it seemed like Daniel might be the one for her. And that irritated her—how could Jason make her question the relationship that had been progressing so nicely?

What right did he have to tell her he loved her, anyway?

She asked herself these questions as she put up chairs and tables Friday evening, preparing for the next day's wedding. The forecast was for dry and sunny—even the humidity was supposed to be under control, but she still worried that one of Kansas's freak storms would move in overnight and rain them out.

She had circumvented the house when she arrived, coming

straight to the backyard. She and Jason had texted a few times to make arrangements during the week, so they both knew what needed to be done, and she had plenty of supplies with her. Others began arriving as they finished up with work, and soon there was a large group helping out.

By the time Jason arrived home and came out to join them, the tables had all been set up and shifted into place, and the chairs for the ceremony were being set up. Jason greeted everyone jointly and got to work, never looking her way.

Adelyn wondered if their relationship was ruined forever—he had been so distant lately, even when they were better at pretending that things were fine. Not that she blamed him, but she just wanted to get back to being friends. What was wrong with the way things had been, anyway?

Somehow they managed to get through the evening without speaking a word directly to each other, and Adelyn pointed her car toward home. Tomorrow was the second wedding, and the last reason for her to spend time with him for a while—unless they ended up at the garden together sometime. Hopefully by then things would have settled down between them.

Adelyn was starting to get anxious Saturday as she stood alone in Jason's kitchen. Where was Maddie, anyway? She and Ben were supposed to have gotten home the night before from their honeymoon, but had car trouble and by the time the car was ready, they decided to get a hotel and stay the night rather than drive home late. But they had only been four hours away, so why weren't they there yet? It was nearly noon.

She looked over at the list of things that needed to be done before the wedding one more time. Bouquets and boutonnieres had been delivered to bride's and groom's rooms—check. Tables decorated—check. Weather report for clear and sunny—check. The last item on her list was the caterer, who should be arriving any moment.

The front door opened and Maddie and Ben walked in, hand-in-hand, still wearing their newlywed glow. "Sorry we're late, we got caught in traffic this morning. There was an accident. Anyway, we're here," Maddie explained.

"Great. Ben, same room as before, will you check in on everyone for me? Maddie, head upstairs. Piper is getting her hair done. I'll be up as soon as the caterer arrives." She had already changed into her dress and had her hair and makeup done. Mostly. The stylist would touch it up when she finished with the other two and the mothers of the bride and groom. The woman was a genius, and very efficient—something Adelyn appreciated.

Another twenty minutes passed and Adelyn had to stop herself from calling to check in with the caterer—she wasn't a big fan of calling people when she knew they should be driving.

Where were they?

"Hey, gorgeous. Look at you." Daniel came in through the sliding glass doors, all debonair—as usual—in his gray pinstripe suit. "You've outdone yourself. Seriously, it looks even better this time than last week. Are you sure you're in the right business?"

She smiled and greeted him with a light kiss. "Thanks, but yes, I'm sure. I'm very happy where I am. Especially when the caterer is running late—I do not need that kind of stress on a regular basis."

There was a knock at the front door and Adelyn headed that direction. It would have been easier if both weddings had used the same caterer, but this company was significantly more expensive than the one Ben and Maddie had chosen, so even though they had reviewed the order three days earlier, they were still a bit of an unknown for her.

"Oh good," Adelyn greeted when she opened the door and saw the caterer standing there with a cart of food. "Come on in." She held her tongue about their lateness, and the caterer made no excuses, even though they had agreed on an arrival time when they had spoken last.

Adelyn showed them where to set up and ran over the plans with them quickly before heading upstairs to the bride's room. The mint-green comforter was covered in dresses, makeup bags, and purses. Despite the chaos in the room, it was still very charming and she was glad Maddie had nudged Jason through the decorating so there was a pretty place to get ready in.

The stylist had finished with Piper—who looked positively stunning—and was just touching up Adelyn's hair when there was a knock at the door.

"Who is it?" Maddie called.

"Me. I need to talk to Adelyn if she can pull herself away," Jason said through the door.

"Just a minute."

"We're about done here, anyway. Your hair is so great."

"She obviously takes good care of her hair." Reece's mother, Elizabeth, gave Maddie a sniff as if to say that hers was far from up to par.

Maddie smiled pleasantly, as if she didn't catch the slight, though Adelyn had no doubt that she had.

A moment later, the stylist pronounced Adelyn finished, and she headed for the door. "I'll be back!"

"I'll be down soon to see if you need any extra help," Maddie said as she sat in front of the stylist. Elizabeth let out a small puff of air that might have been a snide laugh—she had not been impressed with the commoners that Reece had decided to mix with. Adelyn's family had enough money and influence to pass muster, but the rest of them—and most especially Piper—were a far cry from up to snuff, though Elizabeth had stopped making disparaging remarks about Piper—at least to her face—some time ago.

The woman was worse than any bridezilla, too, making both Maddie and Piper seem like angels. Which they practically were, so it wasn't exactly hard.

Adelyn joined Jason in the hall. "What's going on?"

He reached around her to pull the door closed so no one inside could hear, and when he spoke, he kept his voice low. "I think there's a problem with the caterer. Come take a look."

Holy cow, was the nicest thing Adelyn could think when she saw the food they had prepared. It was totally the wrong menu.

"Excuse me, are you sure you have the right wedding?" she asked.

"Of course, 247 Acorn Dr."

"Yes, but this isn't the food the bride and groom ordered." Tacos and tortilla chips—Mrs. Stone would have a heart attack.

"The order clearly states that this is the menu you chose."

"You must be mistaken. Please check the paperwork."

"But ma'am—"

"Did you hear her?" Daniel said, stepping forward.

"Uh, dude, not now." Jason tried to stop him, but Daniel plowed on.

"Obviously if she says there's a problem, then there's a problem. Get the order form."

Adelyn turned toward Daniel, her expression rigidly neutral, though her eyes were furious. "Thanks, but I can handle this."

"I'm just trying to help."

Jason snagged him by the arm and dragged him off, which was a good thing, because otherwise she might have said something very unkind and unwise to the meddlesome man. She sucked in a cleansing breath and turned back to the caterer. "The order form, *please*."

The man hurried to his clipboard and passed it to her. "See, it says clearly that you ordered a taco and nacho bar."

Adelyn flipped back to the front page. "And it says this is for the Sanchez wedding tomorrow, not the Stone/Daniel's wedding *today*. You better get this cleared away and get back with the right food ASAP before Mrs. Stone reams you up one side and down the other. They ordered the salmon puffs, chicken Parmesan and flank steaks. You do have that at your kitchen, right?"

"Of course, except, um, I thought that was tomorrow, so it's not ready."

"Well, you better get it ready. You have no more than three hours until the guests will be wanting food, and if you don't at least have some canapés out, I will be the least of your troubles."

"S-sorry," the man stuttered.

"Just fix it as best you can. Fast." She turned to Jason and Daniel. "Jason, can you grab Ben and help clear this up and get it in the van so he can leave? Give Reece the heads up too. Then we'll need a huddle."

"Of course." Jason headed for his bedroom where the men were dressing, and Daniel started helping the catering staff load unneeded items back into the van.

Adelyn headed up to the bride's suite. "Eve," she said, sticking her head in the room. "Could I talk to you for a moment?"

"Is there a problem?" Maddie asked, her hair half curled.

"No, of course not." Adelyn led Maddie's mom into the hall and closed the door. "We have a problem."

Eve followed her down the stairs. "I kind of guessed. What's up?"

"The caterer brought the wrong food, and he said he thought our food was for tomorrow. If I tell Elizabeth, she'll freak and I don't want her or Piper to know until the ceremony is over. That part, at least, should be flawless, and I don't want it to be marred by catering stress."

"My food handler's permit is still valid from the summer fair. I'd be happy to lend a hand for an hour or two."

"Bless you. They should be ready to head back to their kitchen pretty soon. If it's impossible to get the actual dishes we ordered ready in time, help him put together something that will feed the masses and keep Mrs. Stone's head from completely exploding. I know Reece and Piper will deal if no one else makes a federal case over it."

"Exactly." They entered the kitchen as the men loaded the last of the food into the catering van.

"This is Eve, Jason's mom. She has a food handler's permit and is an excellent cook, and willing to take orders and help you brainstorm an alternative. She's offered to help. Please accept it." Adelyn said to the hand-wringing caterer.

"Yes. Come along. We'll have to figure out a change on the menu, because there isn't time..."

His voice faded out as they headed through the door.

Adelyn slumped against the counter and took a deep breath, then straightened and headed with the guys to the master suite.

"So what's wrong with the caterer?" Reece asked when Adelyn followed the rest of the guys inside.

"There's been a slight mix-up." She explained, and they discussed some alternatives.

"I told mother we should have had Brisket and Noodles do the catering. Okay, well, there's nothing we can do about it right now. We'll see what they come up with, and if we need to call in an emergency order to Graydon, I'm sure he'll be happy to help."

Jason pulled out his phone and sent a text. "I told my mom that's the game plan, so they'll figure it out and make sure there's something to eat when we get through with the ceremony."

Adelyn made a couple of assignments to the guys, checked on their progress for the wedding, and straightened Tony's tie, then headed out again.

"You're amazing, I can't believe how decisive you are, and how well you managed that," Daniel said when they were in the hall.

"Thanks. That's what I do. Can you check with everything outside, to make sure that the florist has what she needs? I need to go check in on everyone in the bride's suite again and make sure they don't know there's a problem."

"Sure thing. What kind of flowers are they supposed to have? Just in case there was another mix-up?" he said in a half-hearted attempt at a joke.

She wasn't worried since the wedding party's flowers had all been right, but she appreciated him asking. "Peach and white roses. Thanks." She gave his arm a quick squeeze and headed up the stairs again. She was still irritated with him for trying to step in when she had the situation under control, but now was not the time to get in to it, so she buried it under layers of calm and smiles before opening the door to check on the bride again.

This time she was able to stay for pre-wedding pictures and a toast to the bride before feeling the need to go downstairs to double-check things below.

She was glad Maddie was there to help smooth things between the mothers of the bride and groom, who disliked each other before they had even met. Though Adelyn had suggested Elizabeth join her son downstairs, she had wanted to be in the bridal suite instead, micromanaging.

The caterer was back, though they didn't open any of the food containers—at Adelyn's request—until after the wedding party had passed through the kitchen, so they wouldn't know there was a small hitch in the plans before the ceremony.

Just before she headed down the aisle on Jason's arm, she saw Graydon Green coming through the door with additional bags of food from Brisket & Noodles.

She let out a long, cleansing breath and turned to Jason. "Shall we?"

"You bet." He looped her arm through his and guided her down the aisle.

Chapter Twenty-six

The ceremony was beautiful—no one could miss how much in love Reece and Piper were as they stood before the priest and spoke their vows. Somehow Tony managed to convince Reece's mom to save her pique about the meal mess-up for a more private moment than the middle of the reception. The final food selections, while not what the bride and groom had chosen, were still delicious. Everything else went smoothly, and after a lovely party—and a wedding dance with the bride and her attendants, that none of them messed up too badly, they were waving to the bride and groom as they drove away in a borrowed convertible with tin cans trailing behind them.

Seeing that Daniel was involved in a business discussion, Adelyn retreated to the bride's room for a few minutes of peace and quiet, to regroup herself and return to being the smiling, open person everyone thought she was naturally. It wasn't that she disliked social activities, but this many hours in a row wore on her energy reserves, especially with the added stress of the food mix up. She packed up the odds and ends left behind in the bag Piper had left with the clothes she had worn there that morning. Next, she wiped down the desk and folded up the chairs Jason had borrowed for the two events.

Adelyn was surprised to encounter Jason on the stairs outside as she headed back to the crowd a few minutes later.

"Hey, I noticed you had disappeared. I wondered if you needed a few minutes of quiet," he said, studying her face.

"You know me so well." Was she that transparent, or was it because he loved her?

Still standing two steps below her, he took her hand and gave it a gentle squeeze. "I do."

It felt for a moment like her hand wasn't the only thing he was touching. Like their connection was so much more—but how could it be? This man meant so much to her—how could she let the relationship they had be lost?

"Adelyn," Daniel's voice called to her from the kitchen area.

Feeling like whatever spell had been weaving between them had broken, Adelyn slowly removed her hand from Jason's. "I'm coming down," she called loud enough for Daniel to hear. Then to Jason, "I cleaned up the bride's room. It'll need a little vacuuming and you'll never be able to tell that it was used as a retreat for womanly beauty."

"Well, that's a relief—we can't have any evidence that women have been here. This is a bachelor pad."

His joke felt flat, but she smiled anyway as she brushed past him on her way down the stairs. She forced the smile wider when Daniel came around the corner and into view.

"There you are. I looked all over for you."

"Sorry, I thought the room where the brides have been primping should be cleaned up before we left, and I needed a moment of quiet."

His brows lifted as he glanced toward the stairs. "Quiet with Jason?"

"No, I was alone. I ran into him only a moment before you called my name. How did you like the reception?"

"There was definitely a different feel to this one than the last.

And a different set of guests." He said it as if the second set was preferable, which was entirely possible from his point of view, since he would know many of them from the bank. Reece had plenty of wealthy and influential contacts.

"It seemed like you had plenty of people to talk to while I was running around with Maddie, seeing to the details. I'm glad." She slid her hand in his, painfully aware of Jason watching them. She gave his hand a tug, heading toward the backyard again.

"Too bad about the catering faux pas. I'm sure Mrs. Stone will bad mouth them all over the city. It'll be hard for them to stay in business."

"Yes." It was a terrible mix up, and Adelyn was still annoyed about the stress it caused her, but she hated to see their business destroyed over it—they had been growing quickly with many happy customers for the past couple of years and their reputation had been impeccable until now.

"Several of the attendees I mentioned it to tonight were appalled."

Now her annoyance shifted. He talked about how Elizabeth would bad-mouth the company, and now he was admitting that he had done so as well. "If you hadn't mentioned it, I'm sure none of the other people here would have realized anything was wrong. The caterers, with a little help, pulled off a terrific save."

"Hmmm, maybe. Do you think Comfrey could get me in to talk to the lottery winners soon? There's a big bonus in it for anyone who gets them to bank at our office. I tried to catch her to talk to her today, but she was very busy with her two swains."

Swains? Who talked like that? "Actually, she's not seeing Tony anymore. The women all know who you are. I'm sure when they figure out what they want to do about their windfall, they'll keep you in mind." Apparently this was nothing but a big business schmooze-fest for him. Why should that bother her?

"Sometimes one has to be pro-active." He shifted directions and headed for the front door. "I need to get back to Ralphie, now that things are winding down here. Most of the guests have left."

"Of course. Thanks for coming with me." She walked him out to his car, parked in a corner of the driveway that had been blocked in for most of the night.

"Dinner at my place tomorrow night?" he asked.

"I...yes, that sounds nice." She had been about to make excuses—things about him were starting to grate on her nerves, but that might have been her exhaustion talking. She would let herself sleep tonight and relax the next morning, and then everything would be better, back to normal again.

Any relationship was bound to have irritations, and she wanted to make this work.

She let him give her a brief kiss goodnight and then she headed back inside to clean up as he drove away.

The last of the guests were meandering slowly toward the gate and their cars as Adelyn, Jason, Ben, Maddie, Tony, Comfrey, Nick, and Jason's parents made a pass through the yard, clearing away debris and saying goodnight to the few stragglers. She didn't miss the fact that parents of both the bride and groom had disappeared as soon as the couple had driven off.

It had been another long week of preparations and Adelyn had been skimping on sleep for days, so she couldn't wait to get home.

When even the others had said goodnight and headed for their cars, she took a final load of tablecloths into the now-finished laundry room to pre-treat stains and start a load.

She loved the efficient layout of the room, the extra rack Jason had installed above the washer that could clip up against the wall, or pull down if he wanted to use it; the handy three-bin separator to keep lights, darks and filthy work clothes for separate loads; and the efficient, large-load washer and dryer they had chosen.

She loved nearly everything about this house.

She started the washer, then exited the room, pulling the door closed behind her.

Jason stood in the kitchen, polishing off a tall glass of water, his tie hanging loosely around his neck and his suit coat unbuttoned.

"I thought you took off with everyone else," he said when he saw her.

"I'm leaving now. I started a load of tablecloths, and the rest are pretreated, but you'll want to rotate the laundry when you get up in the morning."

"Will do." He grabbed a dry erase marker from a cup of writing implements on the counter and scrawled a reminder to himself on a nearby mirror.

"We'll be back to clear away the tables and chairs tomorrow," she said, standing back, knowing she should go, and feeling like an idiot. He had come through in a pinch, as he always did, and really helped make the day run smoother.

"Thanks for everything, from the loan of your beautiful house and yard to your help today. You really made Maddie's and Piper's wedding days special."

"I try."

Unable to help herself, she crossed to him and pulled him into a hug, reveling in the feel of his arms surrounding her, and his cheek resting on the top of her head. Here was comfort in a storm, friendship without strings. She had missed spending time with him since he had said he loved her.

Jason hadn't said a word or hinted about his feelings to her since. Maybe he had realized that he didn't really love her, and that it had been his imagination.

He tightened one arm around her, and used the other to tilt her head up toward his. "Are you still sure there isn't anything but friendship between us?"

The breath caught in her throat and she had to remind herself she was seeing Daniel—and she was not kissing two men in one night. Reluctantly, she pulled back, not sure of her feelings anymore. She told herself it was exhaustion speaking. "I ought to go. But Jason, if you decide to sell this place after you finish up the last room or two, let me know. I love it, and I'd love to live here."

His mouth tightened. "I'll keep that in mind."

She turned and grabbed her purse from a nearby chair. "I'll see you tomorrow."

"Yeah."

Unsettled, she headed for the front door.

A drawer opened and shut in the kitchen as she crossed into the foyer.

"Wait," Jason said, as she turned the nob.

Adelyn turned back to see him crossing the room in two long strides.

"Here. You should have this." He thrust a folded piece of notebook paper at her. "Take it."

"What is it?"

"Your perfect man list. Take it home and look at it again." His jaw bunched as he clenched and unclenched it.

"Okay." Confused, she stashed it in her purse and headed home.

By the time she walked into her place, her brain had already moved on to a dozen other topics and the paper in her purse was long forgotten.

Cleanup at Jason's went smoothly the next afternoon, with plenty of extra hands to stack the tables and chairs into pickup trucks and haul them back to wherever they had come from originally. By the time Adelyn and Maddie vacated Jason's home, it looked better than its pre-wedding condition.

"I bet Jason will be glad to have it back to himself again without us zooming in and out all week," Adelyn said as she put away the final roll of twinkle lights.

"Maybe. I would imagine the place gets lonely sometimes, though. It's so big, and he doesn't need his quiet time the way you do."

Adelyn fit the lid onto the banker's box she had just filled, considering how to say what was on her mind. "He told me he loved me after your bridal shower."

"What? Really? What did you tell him?"

"Honestly, I was stunned. I asked him out a few months ago and he wasn't interested. He seemed almost offended that I would ask him for a date. Not that we don't hang out all the time. I figured he wasn't interested in dating me. Then I've been getting all these hints, but I ignored them because, hello, shut down in March."

"You are such a moron sometimes."

"What?" Adelyn looked up at Maddie in surprise–even a tad offended.

"Did it never occur to you that he said no because you made it obvious that you were only asking him out because of the bet? Maybe he didn't want to date you as part of a bet, maybe he wanted to date you because you liked him that way."

Adelyn went to say something, but her mouth wouldn't work. That hadn't occurred to her–she had thought she was just being honest and straight-forward, but apparently, she was being a jerk. "Oh my gosh. I *am* a moron."

"Luckily, it doesn't happen very often."

"I am such a *moron*." She turned and leaned back against the counter.

Maddie looked at her with a grin. "I love you, Adelyn, even when you're being a moron."

"I guess lucky me, since I've made it a habit all summer." She thought back to everything she and Jason had done together, the food and work and minor disagreements about plant choices. And then the twist of his lips when she had offered to buy the house she had helped him decorate. Somewhere in the back of his mind had he been finishing it for her, was that why he had gotten her opinion so much, or had it just been that he liked her taste? She had always assumed the latter, but maybe she had been wrong.

"Are you all right? You look a little stunned."

"A lot stunned. Major paradigm shift going on here. Do you honestly think he liked me back then?"

"I know he did. He's been wanting to ask you out for over a year, but he was afraid of messing things up between you. Give it a little time to sink in, then you'll know what to do." Maddie patted her on the shoulder, and grabbed a box from the counter, going out to her car.

Adelyn stacked the ones with the lights and headed for her own car, making sure to lock up behind her.

When she got home she was still trying to wrap her head around it all, and trying to come to grips with her own feelings. She thought of their conversations last spring, and into the summer when they talked about her list. Jason had said to look outside the box with it, not to do away with it.

Then she remembered the copy of her list he had given her that she had tucked into her purse. Not that she needed it—but maybe seeing it in black and white would help her see it differently. She put away the lights and then pulled the now-crumpled legal page from her purse, smoothing it out on the counter, and noticed it wasn't just her list, but also some notes of his own down the right-hand side.

1) Ambitious—not willing to just slide by—*I finally got my contractor's license, because only being a framer wasn't enough anymore.*

2) Looks out for what's best for me when I'm not—*sent her home when she had exhausted herself on wedding preparations*

3) Helps me experience new things—*indoor skydiving*

5) Open to new experiences—*tractor pull, anyone?*

6) Will go shopping with me without complaint—*plant shopping with her is a pleasure.*

7) Will step in and help without being asked—*yep*

No need for him to clarify that, he did it all the time.

8) Trusts me to handle my own problems—*anytime.*

She thought of the previous day when he had pulled Daniel away from interfering in her chat with the caterer—he had trusted her to handle it by herself, and then stepped up to do whatever needed to be done when she needed extra hands.

9) Doesn't think an offer of comfort like a hug has to lead to more—*doesn't mean I wouldn't like it to lead to more*

She chuckled at the note.

10) Can handle an adult conversation about feelings

There was no note beside it, but he'd definitely proved it.

11) Isn't afraid to wear either a suit and tie, or to get grubby.—*Check.*

12) Good with his hands—*no question*

13) Likes me for who I am and doesn't try to change me—*why would anyone want to change her?*

14) Loves me and not the idea of me.—*reality is amazing enough already.*

He had said it was her list, but she hadn't realized how well he fit it, how perfectly he filled each condition, had gone out of his way that summer to prove it to her. But it hadn't just been a new effort this summer, those things he had done to fulfill this list were part of his personality, a major part of who he was on the inside.

She leaned against the counter, trying to pull her thoughts together.

A reminder about her dinner with Daniel dinged on her phone and she brought her attention back to her evening plans.

She liked Daniel, and they had a good time together. If she had been so wrong about how well Jason fit her list, maybe she was wrong about Daniel too. She pulled out her notebook and re-wrote the list with Daniel in mind as she answered the questions, thinking surely he would fit it well enough.

She had seldom been so wrong.

Chapter Twenty-seven

When dinner at Daniel's was over and they were enjoying an evening cup of tea after Ralphie was in bed, Adelyn half-listened to Daniel rattle on about interest rates while she compared him again to her list, hoping to find some of the answers were different. No matter how she twisted it, she couldn't quite reconcile some of his actions to her list. But was it really important?

"I thought maybe you could get us into the benefit Mrs. Stone is helping to organize next month. You handle yourself so well in public and we could cut a swath there—plus great business contacts for both of us."

She focused on his words, a little annoyed by them. "I have a number of social engagements that I participate in to help draw business to Crystal Creek, but that one has never been very useful for me. They're mostly big businesses in Kansas City or out of the area. Besides, it's my mother's birthday and we always have a family dinner."

"Surely she would understand your need to attend such an important event. This would be so much bigger. We could be the consummate power couple."

Yeah, the man had ambition, all right. Maybe more than she

wanted. And the fact that he was pushing her into a big public appearance that she had already said she didn't want to do wasn't a point in his favor.

Adelyn tried to remove Jason from the equation as she considered her relationship with Daniel, to look at whether or not they fit as a couple. She couldn't help comparing the two men, though—Daniel wasn't half the man that Jason was, not in any of the areas that really mattered, anyway.

"I don't think this is going to work out."

"Well, if you don't want to go to the benefit, can you still get me a ticket?"

He had such a one-track mind. How had she missed that before? "Yeah, I probably can, but that's not what I meant. I mean us. I don't think we're going to work out."

He paused for a few seconds, as if having to change tracks in his mind. "You're breaking up with me?"

"Yes. I'm sorry. I've tried to make this be the right thing because you're such a great guy, and I really like you. I just don't think we're ever going to have the big L."

"The big L?"

"Love, in all caps, not the way you love a dog or a friend, but real love that can carry you through decades of marriage. I don't think that's in the cards for us."

He blinked in surprise and half stuttered over a couple of his words. "But things are going so well, why can't we ride it out? Is this about Jason? I know he has a thing for you."

Adelyn chuckled. "Yeah, he does and yes, this has something to do with him, though not the way you think. Or at least not completely the way you think." She set the tea cup in her hands onto the trivet beside her. "Here's the thing, I wanted this to work, but it just isn't working for me, despite the fact that you're great and we have fun together."

She steeled herself for honesty, even though she knew it might cause confrontation—which she hated. "I've had blinders on when it came to Jason for quite a while, and I'm ready to take them off. I haven't been dating him." At least she hadn't thought of it as dating. She wasn't so sure anymore. How completely oblivious had she been, anyway? "I've realized that I do have feelings for Jason—ones I've been ignoring all summer. Maybe longer. But even if Jason didn't exist, this thing between us wouldn't make it. I put everything I felt about Jason to the side for the past few weeks so I could focus on us, see if we had a real chance without him in the equation, but I just don't think we do."

Relief poured through her now that the words were out, unchangeable.

Daniel's demeanor did not echo her relief. "So you're saying you had to force yourself to stay in a relationship with me?" He stood. "In that case, you probably better leave."

Regret arched through her as she stood. "That's not what I meant." She could see he wouldn't be mollified, so she didn't continue her explanation. "I wish the best for you."

"Of course." His voice had turned cold, so she retrieved her purse and headed out the door with a goodnight.

Instead of heading home, though, she turned her car toward Jason's house.

Jason had done his best to act normal and unconcerned about Adelyn's presence at his home that day as they finished cleaning up after the weddings. He wasn't sure he had managed to pull it off, but he'd made a valiant effort.

He stepped onto his back porch—he had purchased the strings of Edison lamps that crisscrossed parts of his backyard, and had everyone leave them in place as they pulled down the miles of twinkle lights they had used for the wedding.

He swatted at a mosquito on his arm as he walked down the path he had sweated over as he built it during the summer, but it was perfect. As was the placement of the pergola, and the arrangement of trees, flowers, and bushes. He could imagine them in four or five years when they had grown and filled in spots that were taken up by annuals right now.

Adelyn had been right about all of it.

She always seemed to be right—except when it came to the two of them.

He slumped into a wrought-iron bench she had picked out at a garage sale a few weeks earlier. Also perfect. She could obviously see herself living here just as clearly as she had seen all of this—so why hadn't she been able to see the two of them here, together, the way he did?

He heard the scraping of shoes on pavers and glanced up to see her standing less than ten feet away under the lights, as if magicked there by his thoughts.

"Hi. I rang the doorbell, but you didn't answer, so I thought I'd come on back to see if you were in the yard."

"You found me." He shifted to one side of the bench and patted the empty spot. "What brought you by?"

She didn't sit. He loved the way her blond hair shone like a halo in the lights and waved around her shoulders—she so often wore it up in a bun for work, the buttoned-up business woman. That image appealed as well, but in a different way. She looked serious and for one desperate moment, he wondered if she were there to tell him their friendship had to end.

"I pulled out the list you gave me today. My list. With your notes."

Everything inside him stilled as he waited to hear what she had to say about it. "Yeah?"

"Yeah. It's funny how you can look at something a hundred times and still not see it. Or someone."

He could swear even the cicadas stopped all noise when she said that, in sympathy for the way his heart had all but stopped beating in anticipation. "Don't tease me, Adelyn. I don't think I could take it."

"Okay. Maybe it's time I was a bit more direct, then."

She closed the distance between them and slid onto his lap, brushed her fingers over his five o'clock shadow, and pressed her lips to his.

Finally.

Finally.

Adelyn had been nervous about the bold move, afraid she would be disappointed, but she wasn't. Here was the chemistry her kisses with Daniel had lacked, the zip of electricity that she had felt hints of over the past several weeks. And the home she had been longing for. She slid her fingers through his silky hair.

What had started out as a teasing caress of lips soon shot through all of the other stages of kissing to a thorough exploration that had her heart making up for lost time and blood rocketing through her veins.

She steeped herself in him for several long minutes, his hands in her hair, on her back, tugging her even closer. Then he gentled the kiss to a sweet sharing, and finally, eventually, pulled away. Their eyes locked on each other's and she wished she could read his thoughts there.

"Is that clear enough for you?" she asked when she finally got her voice back.

"I'm not sure I can see clearly when my brain has dribbled out my ears. Give me a moment to see if there's anything left."

She laughed and slid from his lap to the spot on the bench beside him.

He took a moment before asking, "Do I take it that things with you and Daniel are over?"

"Definitely. I looked over the list with your notes and realized that I had been looking everywhere except right in front of me, and that you were right—you are the perfect fit for me."

"So how come you were so blind for so long?" He slid his arm back around her waist.

"Falling for you was not in my plans. I thought I knew how things would work, but you took me by surprise. It shouldn't have been a surprise, because in retrospect, it's so obvious, but sometimes I get a little too tunnel visiony." She hated admitting it, but it was true.

"I've noticed that. So, you came out of the tunnel, and now you're fitting perfectly into my arms."

She slid a hand around his neck. "Like always, only better, because I realized nothing in my life would be half as good without you in it."

Adelyn buried her face in his neck, and though his scent and the feel of his arms around her made her want to kiss him again, she held back.

His voice was a low rumble in her ear. "I don't know when I first started loving you. I just realized one day that you had filled up all the lonely corners of my life, but I didn't know how to tell you."

"I think you did a brilliant job of it." Then she kissed him again and the last thought before her brain completely turned off was that sometimes you couldn't plan the best things in life.

An excerpt from

Last Chance

The final book in the

In The Garden series

Available now!

Comfrey was coming in from a long day of pulling fence—her muscles had been begging for her to quit nearly an hour ago, and she wondered if she would ever get her core temperature back to normal. It was a nastily hot and humid day in Kansas, but she had finished the fence. Finally.

That was good, since she was supposed to pick up the goats in three days and still needed to get their shelter set up in case of a storm. It was all finally coming together. Now she just needed about a gallon of chilled sun tea, a cool shower, and two hours of sitting under the air conditioner.

Coming through the back door of her cottage in town, she chucked her car keys in her shoulder bag and looked up in surprise when the doorbell rang. She wasn't expecting anyone. She brushed the hair back from her face and headed for the door.

Comfrey figured it must be the UPS guy or something—this was about the time he usually made deliveries, but she paused in the act of greeting the visitor when she saw Nicholas Rhodes standing on the other side of the door. He looked entirely too well put together for the heat in his crisp green button-up shirt and tan dress pants—but then, he had always managed to look cool and collected no matter what was going on. "Nick?" Her heart beat slowed and pounded harder than ever in her chest—so hard she could almost hear it.

He shot her his most charming grin. "Hey, Chance, long time, no see."

She realized her mouth was hanging slightly open and closed it. "Yeah, long time. So what brought you to my doorstep?" She desperately wished she could look and sound as cool and relaxed as he did. Instead her two-toned hair was pulled back in a messy bun, her boots were scuffed and muddy from working that day, and she wore some of her scrubbiest clothes. No doubt she positively reeked after six hours in the heat. Perfect, because every woman wanted to run into her ex-fiancé looking like she had just run ten miles in combat boots with wolves nipping at her heels.

"Your mom said she told you I was coming."

It took her a moment to remember the vague text message the previous day. Seeing Nick on her doorstep had fuddled her brain. "Ah, that was the cryptic comment."

"Not so much on the heads up, then?" he asked.

"You know how my mother enjoys her surprises." Comfrey wished Clarissa had been a little more forthcoming this time. And that Nick had called first—surely her mother had given him Comfrey's number if she's given him this address.

"Don't I just?" He peered through the doorway at her living room. "Are you going to invite me in?"

"Oh, yeah, of course. Sorry, I just got in. I've been working outside for most of the day." Comfrey shifted out of the way to make room for him to enter her cozy cottage. She clearly remembered the disdain her mother had shown for it, and wondered what Nick would think. Not that she cared what anyone from her old life thought, but he had always been less snobby than everyone else.

"No problem." He stepped in as she moved away and checked out her place more closely. "I always liked to make you blush, you just come that way in advance this time."

"Lucky me." She still couldn't wrap her head around him being there—but that could be the heat stroke interfering with her brain power. It couldn't be him and his always-compelling person—she was *over* him. Long over.

Nick smiled. "Your mom didn't do this place justice. It's cozy, and totally you."

Her eyes narrowed. "What is that supposed to mean? You never knew this side of me."

He turned to look at her. "Oh, Chance, you only think you suddenly made an about-face."

"Stop calling me that. I go by Comfrey now."

"So I heard. I can't promise not to slip, but I'll try."

"Great. What brings you to town?" It took all her power for Comfrey to keep from wrapping her arms protectively around her waist. She wasn't insecure anymore—not even with Nick—and she refused to act like she was.

"Work. What do you have planned tonight? We should grab some dinner and and catch up."

"I'm vegan now. I know a great place with an all-tofu menu."

She kept her face perfectly bland and felt some pleasure when he blanched. He was a total carnivore, so the lie was maybe a tad more cruel than necessary. "Unfortunately, I have plans tonight. I'm booked for the next several nights, actually. I'm sorry I won't be able to see you while you're in town."

"What do you have going on tonight?" He took her fingers in his, holding her hand lightly in the way of his that implied intimacy without being creepy. It had always weakened her, from the very first date.

But she wasn't going to give in this time. Giving him up the first time had been too hard to do it again.

She wanted to say her plans were a date with her new boyfriend, but despite the very nice kissing she and Tony had enjoyed a couple nights ago, they hadn't made plans for the fair that night. She had never been big on lying, so she told him the truth. "I'm going to the Crystal Creek Founder's Day fair—which actually runs three days now. Several of my friends are involved in events."

His smile widened "Great, I'd love to join you. We might as well eat as long as we're out. What time should I pick you up?"

"Well, the vegan place is over on Stateline, which is a little out of the way."

A muscle in his cheek twitched at her mention of the vegan restaurant again. "Whatever you want. Give me a time to swing back for you."

She decided to have pity on him—he was really willing to take her to a tofu place, even though she knew he hated the stuff with a burning passion. That was one of the many things she had loved about him before. "I think we can probably survive with Chipotle tonight. It's only a few blocks away. I need a long, long shower first, though. Come back for me at six."

His smile softened into something far more natural. "Got it. It's great to see you again, Chance. Comfrey."

"Yeah." She didn't say she was glad to see him, because honestly, she wasn't sure she was glad. She wasn't even sure why she had told him she would go out with him that night instead of telling him to get lost.

Except she owed him a huge apology for dumping him like that four years ago. He deserved better. The real question was why he was being so nice when he was entitled to be bitter and hate her guts. Why would he intentionally seek her out if he was angry about their past, though?

The fact that he was still better looking than Matt Dillon and sweeter than the honey she planned to collect from her bees in a few weeks, would make this visit difficult, but he couldn't be staying more than a few days, so she would live through it, and maybe they would both be able to close that chapter for good.

Get it now!

Acknowledgements

First, thanks to my readers for being so very, very patient for me to finish this series. I hope this story will not disappoint,and promise that book four is on its way!

Big thanks to my beta and grammar readers who made sure that my story was as clean of typos as possible: Patti Hansen, Andrea Simon, Kaylene Zaugg, Diana Shanks, Brooke Heaton, Kayla Batty, Lori Banister, Jen Booth, Tamika Featherstone, Cathy Jeppsen Shellie Davey, and Courtney Hokanson.

Thanks to my partner in crime, Danyelle Ferguson for cheering me on, checking in and encouraging me to finish this story.

And an enormous thanks to my husband Bill, who never ceases to believe in me and support me in everything I do.

About the Author

HEATHER TULLIS has been reading romance for as long as she can remember and has been publishing in the genre since 2009. She has published more than twenty books. When she's not dreaming up new stories to write, or helping out with her community garden, she enjoys playing with her dogs and cat, cake decorating, trying new jewelry designs, inventing new ways to eat chocolate, and hanging out with her husband.

Learn more about her at her website and sign up for her newsletter at http://heathertullis.com/ or her Facebook fan page http://www.facebook.com/HeatherTullisBooks.

Made in the USA
Columbia, SC
05 September 2022

66682777R00126